John Lyly's Endymion, The Man in the Moon: A Retelling

David Bruce

Published by David Bruce, 2022.

JOHN LYLY'S ENDYMION, THE MAN IN THE MOON: A RETELLING

First edition. December 7, 2022.

Copyright © 2022 David Bruce.

ISBN: 979-8215709535

Written by David Bruce.

Table of Contents

Dedication

Dedicated to Carl Eugene Bruce and Josephine Saturday Bruce

My father, Carl Eugene Bruce, died on 24 October 2013. He used to work for Ohio Power, and at one time, his job was to shut off the electricity of people who had not paid their bills. He sometimes would find a home with an impoverished mother and some children. Instead of shutting off their electricity, he would tell the mother that she needed to pay her bill or soon her electricity would be shut off. He would write on a form that no one was home when he stopped by because if no one was home he did not have to shut off their electricity.

The best good deed that anyone ever did for my father occurred after a storm that knocked down many power lines. He and other linemen worked long hours and got wet and cold. Their feet were freezing because water got into their boots and soaked their socks. Fortunately, a kind woman gave my father and the other linemen dry socks to wear.

My mother, Josephine Saturday Bruce, died on 14 June 2003. She used to work at a store that sold clothing. One day, an impoverished mother with a baby clothed in rags walked into the store and started shoplifting in an interesting way: The mother took the rags off her baby and dressed the infant in new clothing. My mother knew that this mother could not afford to buy the clothing, but she helped the mother dress her baby and then she watched as the mother walked out of the store without paying.

My mother and my father both died at 7:40 p.m.

Dedication

Educate Yourself
Read Like A Wolf Eats
Be Excellent to Each Other
Books Then, Books Now, Books Forever

***

In this retelling, as in all my retellings, I have tried to make the work of literature accessible to modern readers who may lack some of the knowledge about mythology, religion, and history that the literary work's contemporary audience had.

Do you know a language other than English? If you do, I give you permission to translate this book, copyright your translation, publish or self-publish it, and keep all the royalties for yourself. (Do give me credit, of course, for the original retelling.)

I would like to see my retellings of classic literature used in schools, so I give permission to the country of Finland (and all other countries) to buy (or get free) one copy of this eBook and give copies to all students forever. I also give permission to the state of Texas (and all other states) to buy (or get free) one copy of this eBook and give copies to all students forever. I also give permission to all teachers to buy (or get free) one copy of this eBook and give copies to all students forever.

Teachers need not actually teach my retellings. Teachers are welcome to give students copies of my eBooks as background material. For example, if they are teaching Homer's *Iliad* and *Odyssey*, teachers are welcome to give students copies of my *Virgil's* Aeneid: *A Retelling in Prose* and tell students, "Here's another ancient epic you may want to read in your spare time."

CAST OF CHARACTERS

Endymion, a young man

Dares, Endymion's page

Eumenides, friend of Endymion

Samias, Eumenides' page

Cynthia, the Goddess of the Moon. Cynthia is the personified Moon.

Tellus, a lady-in-waiting at Cynthia's court. Tellus is a goddess: the personification of Earth.

Floscula, Tellus' woman-servant

Semele, a lady-in-waiting at Cynthia's court

Pythagoras, a Greek philosopher, attendant at Cynthia's court

Gyptes, an Egyptian soothsayer, attendant at Cynthia's court

Panelion, a lord at Cynthia's court

Zontes, a lord at Cynthia's court

Sir Tophas, a braggart

Epiton, Sir Tophas' page. His nickname is "Epi."

Dipsas, an aged sorceress

Bagoa, a sorceress, assistant to Dipsas

Geron, an old man who has experienced hardship

Scintilla, a maid-in-waiting at the court

Favilla, a maid-in-waiting at the court

Three ladies and an ancient (an old) man, in a dumb show

Corsites, a captain

Two Watchmen and a Constable

Four Fairies

Scene: At or near the Court of Cynthia

EDITIONS

Lyly, John. *Endymion*. Edited by George P. Baker. New York: Henry Holt and Company, 1894.

Lyly, John. *Endymion*. Edited by David Bevington. New York: Manchester University Press, 1996.

Lyly, John. *The Plays of John Lyly*. Carter A. Daniel, editor. Lewisburg: Bucknell University Press. London and Toronto: Associated University Presses. 1988.

ONLINE EDITION

Lyly, John. *Endymion*. Modern Spelling - Transcript by B.F. Copyright © 2002

https://sourcetext.com/?s=John+Lyly

https://sourcetext.com/john-lylys-endimion/

LANGUAGE

In this society, a person of higher rank would use "thou," "thee," "thine," and "thy" when referring to a person of lower rank. (These terms were also used affectionately and between equals.) A person of lower rank would use "you" and "your" when referring to a person of higher rank.

The word "wench" at this time was not necessarily negative. It was often used affectionately.

The word "mistress" at this time can mean simply a woman who is loved.

The word "fair" can mean attractive, beautiful, handsome, and good-looking.

"Sirrah" was a title used to address someone of a social rank inferior to the speaker. Friends, however, could use it to refer to each other, and fathers could call their sons "sirrah."

HUMORS

John Lyly's society existed before the age of modern medicine.

Doctors in John Lyly's society believed that the human body had four humors, or vital fluids, that determined one's temperament. Each humor made a contribution to the personality, and one humor could be predominant. For a human being to be sane and healthy, the four humors had to be present in the right amounts. If a man had too much of a certain humor, it would harm his personality and health.

Blood was the sanguine humor. A sanguine man is optimistic.

Phlegm was the phlegmatic humor. A phlegmatic man is calm.

Yellow bile was the choleric humor. A choleric man is angry.

Black bile was the melancholic humor. A melancholic man is gloomy.

A humor can be a disposition.

A humor can be a personal characteristic.

A humor can be a fancy or a whim.

A humor can be a mood.

Cynthia: For Your Information

Cynthia has many names: Diana: Artemis, Phoebe, etc.

One reason for this is that the Greeks and the Romans worshipped goddesses who were similar and so were conflated as one.

Another reason is that Cynthia was a tripartite goddess of the Moon, the Earth, and the Underworld.

Cynthia is a tripartite goddess of the Moon, the Earth, and the Underworld: a goddess with three forms.

• In Heaven, she is Luna, goddess of the Moon. (In this book, the Moon-goddess is called Cynthia.)

• On Earth, she is Diana (Roman name) and Artemis (Greek name), virgin goddess of the hunt.

• In Hell, she is Hecate, goddess of witchcraft.

This book is concerned only with Cynthia the Moon-goddess.

She was born on Mount Cynthus on the island of Delos.

PROLOGUE

The Prologue appeared and addressed Queen Elizabeth I:

"Most high and happy princess, we must tell you a tale of the Man in the Moon, which if it seems ridiculous for the method, or superfluous for the matter, or incredible for the means, for three faults we can make but one excuse: It is a tale about the Man in the Moon.

"It was forbidden in old times to dispute about the chimaera because it was a fiction."

A chimaera is a mythological monster with three heads: one was that of a lion, one was that of a goat, and one was that of a dragon. Its body was also made up of parts of these animals.

"We hope in our times no one will try to match the events and characters of our play with real events and people because the events and characters of our play are imaginative fancies and fantasies; for no one who lives under the sun knows what to make of the Man in the Moon. We present neither comedy, nor tragedy, nor story, nor anything, except something that whosoever hears it may say this:

"'Why, here is a tale of the Man in the Moon.'"

CHAPTER 1

— 1.1 —

Two friends, Endymion and Eumenides, talked together.

Endymion said, "I find, Eumenides, in all things both variety to content and satiety to glut, saving only in my affections, which are so stayed — so hindered — and so stately that I can neither satisfy my heart with love nor my eyes with wonder. My thoughts, Eumenides, are stitched to the stars, which being as high as I can see, thou may imagine how much higher they are than I can reach."

Eumenides said, "If you are enamored of anything above the Moon, your thoughts are ridiculous because immortal things are not subject to affections. If you are allured or enchanted with these transitory things under the Moon, you show yourself senseless to attribute such lofty titles to such low trifles."

"My love is placed neither under the Moon nor above," Endymion said.

"I hope you are not besotted upon and bewitched by the Man in the Moon," Eumenides said.

"No, but I am determined either to die or to possess the Moon herself," Endymion said.

"Is Endymion mad, or am I mistaken?" Eumenides asked. "Do you love the Moon, Endymion?"

"Eumenides, I do love the Moon," Endymion said.

Eumenides said:

"There was never anyone so peevish — so foolish — as to imagine the Moon either capable of affection or capable of the shape of a mistress, for it is as impossible to make love fit her humor — fit her disposition — which no man knows, as it is impossible to fit a coat to her form, which continues not in one bigness while she is being measured."

The size of the Moon continually changes as it goes through its phases.

Eumenides continued:

"Cease, Endymion, to feed so much upon fancies. That melancholy blood must be purged that draws you to a dotage — an infatuation — no less miserable than monstrous."

In this society, melancholy blood was blood that contained too much black bile. A common medical treatment at this time was bloodletting.

Endymion replied, "My thoughts have no veins, and yet, unless my thoughts are let blood, I shall perish."

"But they have vanities that, if they are reformed, you may be restored," Eumenides said.

"Vanities" are vain, unprofitable thoughts. If those thoughts were let go, Endymion could be restored to health.

Endymion said:

"O fair Cynthia, why do others term thee inconstant whom I have always found unmovable?"

Cynthia is the personified Moon.

"Inconstant" means 1) always changing, as in the Moon's cycles, and 2) fickle.

"Unmovable" means 1) constant, and 2) unable to be persuaded.

Endymion continued:

"Injurious time, corrupt manners, unkind men, who, finding a constancy not to be matched in my sweet mistress — my sweet loved one — have christened her with the name of wavering, waxing, and waning!"

The Moon waxes, aka grows, and wanes, aka diminishes, in its cycle.

Endymion continued:

"Is she — the Moon — inconstant who keeps a settled course, which since her first creation has altered not one minute in her moving? There is nothing thought more admirable or commendable in the sea than the ebbing and flowing of the tides; and shall the Moon, from whom the sea takes this virtue, be accounted fickle for increasing and decreasing?

"Flowers in their buds are worth nothing until they have burst out of their buds, nor are blossoms accounted to be worth anything until they are ripe fruit; and shall we then say they are changeable because they grow from seeds to leaves, from leaves to buds, from buds to their perfection?

"Then why aren't twigs that become trees, children who become men, and mornings that grow to evenings termed wavering, because they don't continue in one and the same state?

"Aye, but Cynthia, being in her fullness, decays, as not delighting in her greatest beauty, or withering when she should be most honored. When malice cannot object anything, folly will, making that a vice which is the greatest virtue.

"What thing (my mistress excepted), being in the pride of her beauty and latter minute of her age, grows young again?

"Tell me, Eumenides, who is he who, having a mistress of ripe years and infinite virtues, great honors and unspeakable beauty, would not wish that she might grow tender again, getting youth by the passage of years and getting never-decaying beauty by the passage of time, whose fair face neither the summer's blaze can scorch nor winter's blast chap, nor the numbering of years breed altering of colors?"

Years can change hair color to silver.

Endymion continued:

"Such is my sweet Cynthia, whom time cannot touch because she is divine nor will time offend her because she is delicate.

"O Cynthia, if thou should always continue at thy fullness, both gods and men would conspire to ravish thee. But thou, to abate the pride of our affections, detract from thy perfections, thinking it sufficient if once in a month we enjoy a glimpse of thy majesty; and then, to increase our griefs, thou decrease thy gleams, coming out of thy royal robes, with which thou dazzle our eyes down into thy swath clouts — thy swaddling clothes — beguiling our eyes.

"And then —"

The full Moon wears royal robes, but the Moon decreases until it wears an infant's clothing: swaddling clothes.

Eumenides interrupted, "— stop there, Endymion. Thou who commit idolatry will immediately blaspheme if thou would be allowed. Sleep would do thee more good than speech. The Moon does not hear thee; or if she does, she does not regard and pay attention to thee."

Endymion said:

"Vain, foolish Eumenides, whose thoughts never grow higher than the crown of thy head! Why do thou trouble me, since thou have neither head to conceive the cause of my love nor a heart to receive the impressions that Cynthia has made on my heart?

"Follow thou thine own fortunes, which creep upon the earth, and allow me to fly to mine, whose fall, although it is desperate, yet it shall come by daring.

"Farewell."

Endymion exited.

Now alone, Eumenides said to himself:

"Without doubt Endymion is bewitched; otherwise, in a man of such rare — uncommon and splendid — virtues, there could not harbor a mind of such extreme madness.

"I will follow him, lest in this fancy of the Moon, he deprives himself of the sight of the Sun by committing suicide."

— 1.2 —

Tellus and Floscula talked together. Tellus was a lady-in-waiting at Cynthia's court, and Floscula was Tellus' waiting-woman. Tellus was a goddess: the personification of Earth.

Tellus loved Endymion, but Endymion loved Cynthia.

Tellus said:

"Treacherous and most perjured Endymion, is Cynthia the sweetness of thy life and the bitterness of my death? What revenge may be devised so full of shame as my thoughts are plenished and equipped with malice?

"Tell me, Floscula, whether falseness in love can possibly be punished with extremity of hate. As long as sword, fire, or poison may be hired, no traitor to my love shall live unrevenged."

Tellus then addressed Endymion, who was not present, in an apostrophe:

"Were thy oaths without number, thy kisses without measure, thy sighs without end, forged to deceive a poor credulous virgin whose simplicity had been worth thy favor and better fortune? If the gods sit as unequal beholders of injuries or laughers at lovers' deceits, then let revengeful evil be as well forgiven in women as perjury is winked at in men."

Floscula said, "Madam, if you would compare the state of Cynthia with your own, and the height of Endymion's thoughts with the meanness — the lowliness — of your fortune, you would rather yield than contend and compete, since there is between you and her no comparison, and you would rather wonder than rage at the greatness of his mind, being affected by and afflicted by and in love with a thing more than mortal: Cynthia."

"No comparison, Floscula?" Tellus said. "And why so? Isn't my beauty divine, whose body is decked with fair flowers, and whose veins are vines, yielding sweet liquor to the dullest spirits, whose ears are corn and wheat to bring strength, and whose hairs are grass to bring abundance? Doesn't frankincense and myrrh breathe out of my nostrils, and all the sacrifice to the gods breed in my bowels? Infinite are my creatures, without which neither thou nor Endymion nor anyone could love or live."

Tellus was the goddess of the earth.

Floscula said:

"But don't you know, fair lady, that Cynthia governs all things? Your grapes would be only dry husks, your corn and wheat would be only chaff, and all your virtues — all your powers — would be only vain if not for Cynthia, who preserves the one in the bud and nourishes the other in the blade [aka leaf of a plant; 'in the blade' means 'only leaf, not yet in ear'], and who by her influence comforts all things and who by her authority commands all creatures.

"Allow then Endymion to follow his affections, although to obtain her is impossible, and let him flatter himself in his own imaginations because they are concerned with Cynthia, who is immortal."

Tellus said to the absent Endymion:

"Loath I am, Endymion, that thou should die, because I love thee well, and it grieves me that thou should live, because thou love Cynthia too well. In these extremities, what shall I do?"

She then said:

"Floscula, no more words. I am resolved: He shall neither live nor die."

"A strange practice — a strange trick — if it is possible," Floscula said.

Tellus said:

"Yes, it is possible. I will entangle him in such a sweet net that he shall neither find the means to come out nor desire it. All allurements of pleasure I will cast before his eyes, insomuch that he shall slake and slack that love which he now vows to Cynthia and he shall burn in love of me, for whom he seems not to care.

"In this languishing between my amorous devices and his own loose desires, such dissolute thoughts shall take root in his head, and over his heart shall grow so thick a skin, that neither hope of preferment nor fear of punishment, nor counsel of the wisest nor company of the worthiest shall alter his humor — his disposition — nor make him once think of his honor."

"This is a revenge incredible, and if it may be put in action, it is unnatural: It is supernatural and cruel," Floscula said.

Tellus said:

"He shall know that the malice of a woman has neither mean nor end, and he shall know that a woman deluded in love has neither rule nor reason. I can do it. I must. I will. All his virtues I will shadow with vices; his person — ah, his sweet person! His sweet body! — he shall deck with such rich robes that he shall forget it is his own person; his sharp wit — ah, wit too sharp, that has cut off all my joys! — he shall use in flattering my face and devising sonnets in my favor.

"The prime of his youth and the pride and flower of his time shall be spent in melancholy passions, careless behavior, untamed thoughts, and unbridled affections."

"When this is done, what then?" Floscula asked. "Shall it continue until his death, or shall he dote forever in this delight?"

"Ah, Floscula, thou rend my heart in sunder. Thou split my heart apart in putting me in remembrance of the end," Tellus said.

Endymion was mortal, and someday he would die. Tellus was immortal, and always she would live.

"Why, if this is not the end, then all the rest is to no end — to no purpose," Floscula said.

"Yet allow me to imitate Juno, who would turn Jupiter's lovers to beasts on the earth, although she knew afterwards they would be stars in heaven," Tellus said.

Juno's husband, Jupiter, raped Callisto. Juno, who hated the women whom her husband slept with, even when they were raped, turned Callisto into a bear. Years later, Callisto saw her son, Arcas, who prepared to defend himself with a spear against what he thought was a bear. Jupiter turned Arcas and Callisto into constellations. Callisto became Ursa Major: Big Bear. Arcas became Ursa Minor: Little Bear.

Floscula said, "Affection that is bred by enchantment is like a flower that is wrought in silk: in color and form most similar, but not at all similar in substance or smell."

Love potions may work, but the love that results is not true love.

Tellus said, "Affection that is bred by enchantment shall suffice for me, if the world gossips that I am favored by Endymion."

Floscula replied, "Well, use your own will, but you shall find that love gotten with witchcraft is as unpleasant as fish that is taken — captured — with unwholesome medicines."

Tellus said:

"Floscula, they who are so poor that they have neither net nor hook will rather poison dough — catch fish with poison bait — than pine with hunger; and she who is so oppressed with love that she is able neither with beauty nor with wit to obtain her friend — her lover — will rather use unlawful means than experience intolerable pains.

"I will do it."

She exited.

Alone, Floscula said to herself:

"Then go about it.

"Poor Endymion, what traps are laid for thee because thou honor one whom all the world marvels at! And what plots are cast to make unfortunate thee who studies of all men to be the most faithful!"

Dares and Samias talked together. Dares was Endymion's page, and Samias was Eumenides' page. Pages are boy-servants.

Dares said, "Now that our masters are in love up to the ears, what do we have to do but to be in knavery over the ears and up to the crowns of our head?"

Of course, Endymion was in love with Cynthia. Soon we will learn that Eumenides was in love with Semele.

Samias said:

"O, I wish that we had Sir Tophas, that 'brave' squire, in the midst of our mirth.

"And *ecce autem* — lo and behold — you will see the devil!"

A proverb stated, "Speak of the devil, and he will appear."

Sir Tophas and Epiton entered the scene. Sir Tophas was a braggart, and Epiton was Sir Tophas' page. Epiton's nickname was "Epi."

Sir Tophas said, "Epi?"

"Here, sir," Epiton said.

"I cannot endure this idle humor — this idle feeling — of love," Sir Tophas said. "It does not tickle my liver, from whence the love-mongers in former ages seemed to infer it should proceed."

The ancients thought that the liver was the seat of love; we tend to think the heart is.

Epiton said, "Love, sir, may lie in your lungs, and I think it does; and that is the reason you pant and puff and are so pursy — so short-winded."

"Tush, boy, I think it is just some device of the poet to get money," Sir Tophas said.

"A poet?" Epiton said. "What's that?"

"Don't thou know what a poet is?" Sir Tophas asked.

"No," Epiton said.

Sir Tophas "explained":

"Why, fool, a poet is as much as one would say, a poet."

Seeing Samias and Dares, he said:

"But wait, yonder are two wrens. Shall I shoot at them?"

"They are two lads," Epiton said.

"Larks or wrens, I will kill them," Sir Tophas said.

"Larks? Are you blind?" Epiton said. "They are two little boys."

"Birds or boys, they are both but a pittance for my breakfast," Sir Tophas said. "Therefore, have at them, for their brains must, as it were, embroider — decorate — my bolts."

"Have at them" is a declaration of a readiness to fight.

Bolts are arrows.

Sir Tophas took aim at Samias and Dares.

Samias said to Sir Tophas, "Stay — calm — your courage, valiant knight, for your wisdom is so weary that it stays — stops short — itself."

Dares said, "Why, Sir Tophas, have you forgotten your old friends?"

"Friends?" Sir Tophas said. "*Nego argumentum* — I reject your argument."

"And why aren't we your friends?" Samias asked.

Sir Tophas said:

"Because, *amicitia*, as in old annals we find, is *inter pares*."

Annuals are records of events year by year.

Amicitia inter pares means "friendship among equals."

Sir Tophas continued:

"Now my pretty companions, you shall see how unequal you are to me."

He measured himself against them by standing close to them.

Sir Tophas then said:

"But I will not cut you quite off; you shall be my half-friends, for you reach only to my middle. So far as from the ground to the waist, I will be your friend."

Dares said:

"Learnedly."

"Learnedly" means "in a learned manner."

Dares then asked:

"But what shall become of the rest of your body, from the waist to the crown?"

Normally, the learned half is from the waist to the crown, as the head contains the brain. But Sir Tophas' brain was so lacking that his learned half was from the waist to the feet.

Sir Tophas answered, "My children, *quod supra vos nihil ad vos* — that which is higher than you is nothing to you — you must think the rest immortal because you cannot reach it."

Epiton said to Samias and Dares, "Nay, I tell you, my master is more than a man."

Dares said to Epiton, "And thou are less than a mouse."

"But who are you two?" Sir Tophas asked.

"I am Samias, page to Endymion," Samias said.

"And I am Dares, page to Eumenides," Dares said.

"Of what occupation are your masters?" Sir Tophas asked.

"Occupation, you clown?" Dares said. "Why, they are honorable, and they are warriors."

"Occupation" can refer to menial work.

"Then they are my apprentices," Sir Tophas said.

"Thine?" Dares said. "And why so?"

Sir Tophas said:

"I was the first who ever devised war, and therefore Mars himself gave me for my arms a whole armory, and thus I go as you see, clothed with artillery.

"It is not silks (a favorite material for milksops), nor tissues, nor the fine wool of *Seres*, but iron, steel, swords, flame, shot, terror, clamor, blood, and ruin that rock asleep my thoughts, which never had any other cradle but cruelty."

"Tissues" are fine cloths.

Seres is the Latin word for an area of eastern Asia, the inhabitants of which were reputed to have fine wool.

Sir Tophas then said:

"Let me see, don't you bleed?"

"Why would I bleed?" Dares asked.

"Commonly my words wound," Sir Tophas said.

"What then do your blows?" Samias asked.

"They not only wound, but also confound and destroy," Sir Tophas said.

Samias asked Epiton:

"How dare thou come so near thy master, Epi?"

He then said:

"Sir Tophas, spare us."

Sir Tophas said, "You shall live. You, Samias, shall live because you are little; you, Dares, shall live because you are no bigger; and both of you shall live, because you are only two; for commonly I kill by the dozen, and I have for every particular adversary a peculiar weapon."

"Peculiar" means 1) particular, and 2) badly suited.

He displayed his weapons.

"May we know the use, for our better skill in war?" Samias asked.

"You shall," Sir Tophas said. "Here is a bird-bolt for the ugly beast known as the blackbird."

As Sir Tophas mentioned each of his weapons, he displayed it.

Bird-bolts are blunt arrows for shooting birds.

"A cruel sight," Dares said.

Sir Tophas said, "Here is the musket for the untamed, or (as the vulgar sort term it) the wild, mallard."

He demonstrated, not heeding them as they talked.

"O desperate attempt!" Samias said.

"Nay, my master will be a match for them," Epiton said.

Sir Tophas was a match for a duck — no duck would defeat him.

Dares said, "Aye, if he catches them."

Sir Tophas said, "Here are spear and shield, and both are necessary: the one to conquer, the other to subdue or overcome the terrible trout, which, although he is under the water, yet tying a string to the top of my spear and an engine of iron to the end of my line, I overthrow him, and then herein I put him."

The "engine of iron" is a fishhook. He can tie a fishing line to his spear, and he can use his shield to carry any fish he catches.

He showed his gear and strutted about, oblivious to their talk.

Samias said out loud:

"O wonderful war!"

He then whispered:

"Dares, have thou ever heard such a dolt?"

Dares whispered, "All the better. We shall have good sport and entertainment hereafter if we can get leisure."

Samias whispered:

"Leisure! I would rather lose my master's service than his company. Look at how he struts."

He was willing to shirk his duty and risk getting fired than to lose the opportunity of seeing Sir Tophas make a fool of himself.

Samias then said out loud to Sir Tophas:

"But what is this? Do you call it your sword?"

Sir Tophas answered, "No, it is my scimitar, which I, by construction often studying to be compendious, call my smiter."

"Compendious" means "concise," but "concise" is a more concise word than "compendious."

"What! Are you also learned, sir?" Dares asked.

"Learned?" Sir Tophas said. "I am all Mars and *Ars*."

Mars is the god of war. *Ars* is Latin for "the arts."

"Nay, you are all mass and ass," Samias said.

Sir Tophas said:

"Do you mock me? You shall both suffer; yet you shall be killed by such weapons as you shall make choice of. Am I all mass or lump — is there no proportion in me? Am I all ass — is there no wit and intelligence in me?

"Epi, prepare them for the slaughter."

In other words, give them their choice of weapons to be killed by.

Samias said, "Please, sir, hear us speak. We call you 'mass,' which your learning well understands is all 'man,' for *mas, maris*, is a man. Then *as*, as you know, is a weight; and we for your virtues account you a weight."

Mas, maris is Latin for "male."

An *as* was a unit of weight in Roman times.

Hmm. "We for your virtues account you a weight." What kind of weight? Probably a dead weight.

Sir Tophas said, "The Latin has saved your lives — lives that a world of silver could not have ransomed. I understand you and pardon you."

In this society, a person who could read Latin could be saved from being hung, as religious people such as priests knew Latin and could be excused from being sentenced by a secular court. This was called benefit of clergy.

"Well, Sir Tophas, we bid you farewell," Dares said, "and at our next meeting we will be ready to do you service."

Sir Tophas said:

"Samias, I thank you.

"Dares, I thank you.

"But especially I thank you both."

Samias said:

"Wisely."

Well, thoroughly.

Samias then said to Dares, "Come, next time we'll have some pretty gentlewomen to walk with us, for without doubt he will be very dainty with them."

"Dainty" means pleasant and debonair. But Sir Tophas would also be a sweet target for the wit of the ladies.

Dares whispered to Samias, "Come, let us see what our masters are doing; it is high time we did that."

Dares and Samias exited.

Sir Tophas said, "Now I will march into the field, where, if I cannot encounter with my foul — and fowl — enemies, I will withdraw myself to the river and there fortify myself with weapons to fight fish; for no minute rests free from fight."

Sir Tophas and Epiton exited.

— 1.4 —

Tellus and Floscula entered the scene from one direction; Dipsas entered the scene from another direction.

Dipsas was an aged sorceress.

Tellus said, "Look, Floscula, we have met with the woman by chance whom we sought by travel and travail. I will break my mind to her without ceremony or circumstance, lest we lose time in advice that should be spent in execution. I will tell her what I want simply and quickly."

Floscula said, "Use your discretion. I will in this case neither give counsel nor consent; because there cannot be a thing more monstrous than to force affection by sorcery, and I do not imagine anything more impossible."

Tellus said:

"Tush, Floscula, in obtaining love what impossibilities will I not try? And for the winning of Endymion, what impieties will I not practice?"

She went to Dipsas and said:

"Dipsas, whom as many honor for age as marvel at for cunning, listen to my tale of few words and answer in one word to the purpose — yes or no — because my burning desire cannot afford long speech nor can the short time I have to stay afford many delays.

"Is it possible by herbs, stones and minerals, spells, incantation, enchantment, exorcisms, fire, metals, planets, or any plot or trick, to plant affection where it is not and to supplant it where it is?"

Dipsas said:

"Fair lady, you may imagine that these hoary hairs are not void of experience, and you may imagine that the great name and reputation that goes abroad about my cunning is not without cause or reason.

"I can darken the Sun by my skill and move the Moon out of her course; I can restore youth to the aged and make hills without bottoms.

"There is nothing I cannot do except only that which you would have me do, and therein I differ from the gods, in that I am not able to rule hearts; for, if it were in my power to place affection by appointment, I would make such evil appetites, such inordinate lusts, such cursed desires that all the world would be filled both with superstitious and credulous passions and with extreme love."

Tellus said to herself, "Unhappy Tellus, whose desires are so desperate that they are neither to be conceived by any creature nor to be cured by any art!"

Dipsas said:

"This I can do: Breed slackness in love although I can never root it out.

"Who is he whom you love, and who is she whom he honors?"

Tellus said, "Endymion, sweet Endymion, is he who has my heart; and Cynthia — too, too fair Cynthia — the miracle of nature, of time, of fortune, is the lady whom he delights in, and dotes on every day and dies for ten thousand times a day."

"Do you wish to have his love made slack either by absence or sickness?" Dipsas asked. "Do you wish that Cynthia should openly mistrust him or openly be jealous of him without reason or excuse?"

Tellus said:

"It is the only thing I crave.

"Seeing that my love to Endymion, unspotted, cannot be accepted, I crave that his truthful allegiance to Cynthia, although it is inexpressible in words, may be doubted."

Dipsas said, "I will undertake it and overtake — overcome — him, so that all his love shall be doubted and therefore he shall be in despair. But this will wear out with time, which treads all things down but truth."

Her spell would wear out, and possibly Endymion's love for Cynthia would wear out — that is, weather — the metaphorical storm created for him by Dipsas at Tellus' request.

"Let us go," Tellus said.

"I follow," Dipsas said.

All exited.

CHAPTER 2

— 2.1 —

Alone, Endymion said to himself:

"O fair Cynthia! O unfortunate Endymion! Why wasn't thy birth as high as thy thoughts, or her beauty less than heavenly? Or why aren't thine honors as rare and splendid as her beauty or thy fortunes as great as thy deserts?

"Sweet Cynthia, how would thou be pleased? How would thou be possessed? Will labors, patient of and enduring all extremities, obtain thy love? There is no mountain so steep that I will not climb it, no monster so cruel that I will not tame it, no action so desperate that I will not attempt to do it.

"Do thou desire the passions of love, the sad and melancholy moods of perplexed minds, the not-to-be-expressed torments of racked — pulled this way and then pulled that way — thoughts? Behold my sad tears, my deep sighs, my hollow eyes, my broken sleeps, my heavy countenance.

"Would thou have me vowed only to thy beauty and consume every minute of time in thy service? Remember my solitary life, almost these seven years."

Seven years were the length of an apprenticeship. Endymion had spent almost seven years loving Cynthia.

Endymion continued:

"Whom have I entertained except my own thoughts and thy virtues? What company have I had but contemplation? Whom have I wondered at but thee? Nay, whom have I not contemned and disdained for thee?

"Haven't I crept and abased myself to those on whom I might have trodden, only because thou shined upon them? Haven't injuries been sweet to me if thou vouchsafe and permit that I should bear them? Haven't I spent my golden years in hopes, growing old with wishing, yet wishing nothing except thy love?

"With Tellus, fair Tellus, I have dissembled and put on a false front, using her only as a cloak for my affections, so that others, seeing my mangled and disordered mind, might think it were for one who loves me, not for Cynthia, whose perfection allows no companion or comparison.

"In the midst of these distempered and vexed thoughts of mine, thou are not only doubtful about my truth, but indifferent, mistrustful, and safe and secure from my passion, which strange humor — strange disposition — makes my mind as desperate as thy conceits and fancies are difficult to discern."

Endymion loved Cynthia deeply; Cynthia mostly ignored him.

Endymion continued:

"I am not one of those wolves that bark most when thou shine brightest."

Wolves bark at that which they cannot hurt. They are analogous to petty, jealous underlings who "bark" because they are jealous of others' accomplishments.

Endymion continued:

"But I am that fish — thy fish, Cynthia, in the flood Araris [a river] — which at thy waxing is as white as the driven snow and at thy waning is as black as deepest darkness.

"Sweet Cynthia, I am that Endymion, who has carried my thoughts in equal balance with my actions, being always as free from imagining ill as I am free from endeavoring to commit ill.

"I am that Endymion whose eyes never esteemed anything fair except thy face, whose tongue called nothing rare and splendid except thy virtues, and whose heart imagined nothing miraculous except thy government — thy conduct and thy rule.

"Yes, I am that Endymion who, divorcing himself from the amiableness of all ladies, the bravery — the splendor — of all courts, the company of all men, has chosen in a solitary cell to live only by feeding on thy favor, accounting nothing excellent, nothing immortal in the world — except thyself.

"Thus may thou see every vein, sinew, muscle, and artery of my love, in which there is no flattery nor deceit, no error nor artfulness.

"But wait, here comes Tellus. I must turn my other face to her like Janus, lest she be as suspicious as Juno."

Janus is a two-faced god.

Juno was the jealous — with good reason — wife of Jupiter, King of the gods.

Tellus, Floscula, and Dipsas entered the scene.

Tellus said:

"Yonder I see Endymion. I will seem to suspect nothing, but soothe him, so that seeing I cannot obtain the depth of his love, I may learn the height of his dissembling.

"Floscula and Dipsas, withdraw yourselves out of our sight, yet be within the hearing of our greetings to each other."

Floscula and Dipsas withdrew.

Tellus then said:

"How are you now, Endymion? Always solitary? No company but your own thoughts? No friend but melancholy fancies?"

Endymion said, "You know, fair Tellus, that the sweet remembrance of your love is the only companion of my life, and thy presence is my paradise, so that I am not alone when nobody is with me, and I am in heaven itself when thou are with me."

"Then you love me, Endymion?" Tellus asked.

"Or else I don't live, Tellus," Endymion answered.

This is ambiguous. It can mean that he cannot live without her love, or that she will kill him if she finds out that he loves someone else.

"Isn't it possible for you, Endymion, to dissemble?" Tellus asked.

"Not, Tellus, unless I could make me a woman," Endymion answered.

This is ambiguous. It can mean that Endymion would dissemble to Tellus if he could make himself into a woman. But the word "make" can also mean "To pair, match, mate with," according to the *Oxford English Dictionary*. If Endymion could pair himself with Cynthia, as he does in his imagination, then he would dissemble to Tellus, as in fact he is doing.

"Why, is dissembling joined to their sex inseparably, as heat to fire, heaviness to earth, moisture to water, thinness to air?" Tellus asked.

"No, but dissembling is found in their sex as common as spots upon doves, moles upon faces, caterpillars upon sweet apples, cobwebs upon fair windows," Endymion answered.

Mourning doves have black spots on their wings, as do common ground-doves.

"Do they all dissemble?" Tellus asked.

"All but one," Endymion answered.

"Who is that?" Tellus asked.

"I dare not tell you," Endymion answered. "For if I should say it were you, then you would imagine my flattery to be extreme; if I say it was another, then you would think my love to be only indifferent."

Tellus said:

"You will be sure I shall take no advantage of and gain no profit from your words."

An additional meaning of Tellus' words is that Endymion is choosing his words carefully so that he is hiding his love for Cynthia: a love that is of no advantage to Tellus.

Tellus continued:

"But tell the truth, Endymion, without standing on ceremonies and formalities: Isn't it Cynthia?"

Endymion said, "You know, Tellus, that we are forbidden to dispute about the gods because their deities don't come within the compass of our reasons; and we are not allowed to talk about Cynthia except to marvel, because her virtues are not within the reach of our capacities."

"Why, she is only a woman," Tellus said.

"No more was Venus," Endymion said.

Venus, sexually active goddess of sexual passion, was renowned for beauty.

"She is only a virgin," Tellus said.

"No more was Vesta," Endymion said.

Vesta, virgin goddess of the hearth, was renowned for chastity.

"She shall have an end," Tellus said.

"So shall the world," Endymion said.

"Isn't her beauty subject to time?" Tellus asked.

"No more than time is subject to standing still," Endymion said.

"Will thou make her immortal?" Tellus asked.

"No, but she is incomparable," Endymion said.

Cynthia, the Moon goddess, was immortal, but Queen Elizabeth I was often called Cynthia in allegories.

Tellus said:

"Take heed, Endymion, lest like the wrestler in Olympia who, striving to lift an impossible weight, caught an incurable strain, thou by fixing thy thoughts above thy reach fall into a disease without all recovery and cure.

"But I see thou are now in love with Cynthia."

Endymion said:

"No, Tellus, thou know that the stately cedar, whose top reaches to the clouds, never bows his head to the shrubs that grow in the valley; and you know that ivy, which climbs up by the elm, can never get hold of the beams of the Sun.

"I in all humility honor Cynthia, whom none ought or dare venture to love, whose affections are immortal and whose virtues are infinite.

"Allow me, therefore, to gaze on the Moon, at whom, were it not for thyself, I would die with marveling."

Dares, Samias, Scintilla, and Favilla talked together. Dares and Samias were pages, and Scintilla and Favilla were maids-in-waiting at the court.

Dares said, "Come, Samias, did thou ever hear such a sighing: the one for Cynthia, the other for Semele, and both for Moonshine in the water?"

Endymion loved Cynthia, and Eumenides loved Semele.

People who love Moonshine in the water love something that will not return their love.

Samias said:

"Let them sigh and let us sing.

"What do you say, gentlewomen, aren't our masters too far gone in love?"

Scintilla said, "Their tongues are happily dipped to the root in amorous words and sweet discourses, but I think their hearts are scarcely tipped — lightly touched — on the side with constant desires."

Dares said, "What do you say, Favilla? Isn't love a lurcher — a petty thief, that takes away men's stomachs with the result that they cannot eat, takes away their spleen with the result that they cannot laugh, takes away their hearts with the result that they cannot fight, takes away their eyes with the result that they cannot sleep, and leaves nothing but livers to make nothing but lovers?"

This society regarded the liver as the site of love.

"Away, peevish boy," Favilla said. "A rod would be better under thy belt than love in thy mouth. It will be a forward, presumptuous cock that crows in the shell."

Hmm. A rod under a man's belt? Bawdy, that.

Favilla was saying that Dares was too young to be concerned about such things as having his belt at his knees.

Dares said, "Alas, good old gentlewoman, how it becomes you to be grave!'

He was mocking her; Favilla was a young virgin.

Scintilla said, "Favilla, although she is only a spark, yet she is fire."

"And you, Scintilla, are not much more than a spark, although you would be esteemed a flame," Favilla said.

Samias whispered to Dares, "It would be good entertainment to see the fight between two sparks."

Dares whispered to Samias, "Let them go at it, and we will warm ourselves by their words."

"You are not angry, Favilla?" Scintilla asked.

"That is, Scintilla, as you wish to take it," Favilla said. "Take it as you wish."

Samias said, "That! That!"

In other words: Go at it, girls! Or: Sic 'em!

Scintilla said, "This it is to be matched with girls, who, coming but yesterday from the making of babies, would before tomorrow be accounted matrons."

One meaning of "babies" is "dolls."

But these babies may be real babies.

Matrons are married women, especially older married women with large families.

Favilla said, "I beg your matronship's mercy and pardon. Because your pantofles are higher with cork, your feet must therefore be higher in the insteps. You will pretend to be my elder because you stand upon a stool, and I stand on the floor."

Scintilla was perhaps a little older and a little taller than Favilla, at least when Scintilla was wearing shoes with raised heels.

Favilla was accusing Scintilla of being proud. "Pantofles" are slippers with raised heels; Favilla called Scintilla's raised heels a stool. A person who is proud is high in the insteps.

Entertained by the fight, Samias said, "Good! Good!"

Dares whispered to Samias, "Let them alone, and see with what countenance they will become friends."

They could become friends, or they could become "friends."

Scintilla said to Favilla, "You think that you are the wiser of us because you mean to have the last word."

The two young women threatened each other.

Samias whispered to Dares, "Step between them lest they scratch."

Samias then said out loud to Scintilla and Favilla, "In truth, gentlewomen, seeing we came out to be merry, don't let your jarring and fighting mar our jests. Be friends. What do you say?"

"I am not angry, but it spited me to see how short and abrupt she was," Scintilla said.

"I meant nothing hurtful until she found it necessary to cross me," Favilla said.

"Then so let it rest," Dares said.

"I am agreed," Scintilla said.

Weeping, Favilla said, "And I ... yet I never took anything so unkindly in all my life."

Weeping, Scintilla said, "It is I who have the cause and reason to weep, although I never offered the occasion for a fight."

"Excellent, and exactly like a woman," Dares said.

"It is a strange sight to see water come out of fire," Samias said.

"It is women's nature to carry in their eyes fire and water, tears and torches, and in their mouths, honey and gall," Dares said.

Scintilla said:

"You will be a good one if you live. Yes, if you escape the gallows, you will be a fine man.

"But who is yonder formal fellow?"

Sir Tophas' appearance was formal. He presented the essence as well as the appearance of a type of man: one who loved weapons but who had a better opinion of himself than other people had of him. He was the essence of a *miles gloriosus*: a comic boastful soldier.

Sir Tophas and Epiton entered the scene.

Dares whispered to Scintilla and Favilla, "He is Sir Tophas, Sir Tophas about whom we told you. If you are good wenches, pretend as if you love him and marvel at him."

"We will do our parts," Favilla said.

Dares said, "But first let us stand aside and let him use his garb and show his style, for all our entertainment consists in his gracing us by showing what kind of man he is."

The pages and maids-in-waiting stood to the side, unnoticed, in order to watch Sir Tophas make a fool of himself.

Sir Tophas said, "Epi!"

"At hand, sir," Epiton said.

Sir Tophas asked, "How do thou like this martial life, where nothing but blood besprinkles our bosoms? Let me see, are our enemies fat?"

His enemies were the fish, fowl, and animals he fished or hunted — or, as he would say, battled.

Epiton said, "Surpassingly fat. And I would not change this life to be a lord, and you yourself surpass all comparison; for other captains kill and beat, and there is nothing you kill but you also eat."

"Surpass all comparison" means 1) are without equal, or 2) are too foolish and outlandish for words.

Sir Tophas said, "I will draw their guts out of their bellies, and tear the flesh with my teeth, so mortal and deadly is my hate and so eager my unstaunched stomach."

"Stomach" can mean 1) courage, or 2) hunger.

Epiton said to himself, "My master thinks himself the most valiant man in the world if he kills a wren, so warlike a thing he accounts it to take away life, although it be from a lark."

Sir Tophas said, "Epi, I find my thoughts to swell and my spirit to take wings, insomuch that I cannot continue within the compass of so slender combats."

"This surpasses all our expectations! This surpasses belief!" Favilla whispered.

"Why, isn't he mad?" Scintilla whispered.

"No, he is only a little vainglorious and proud," Samias said.

Sir Tophas said, "Epi!"

"Sir?" Epiton responded.

Sir Tophas said, "I will encounter that black and cruel enemy that bears rough and untewed — uncombed — locks upon his body, whose sire throws down the strongest walls, whose legs are as many as both ours, on whose head are placed most horrible horns by nature as a defense from all harms."

"What do you mean, master, to be so desperate?" Epiton asked.

It certainly sounds as if a battle against such an enemy would be a desperate encounter.

Sir Tophas said, "Honor incites me, and hunger itself compels me."

The hunger is for honor — and for food.

"What is that monster?" Epiton asked.

Sir Tophas said, "The monster *ovis*. I have said the word: Let thy wits work."

Epiton said, "I cannot imagine it. Yet let me see. A black enemy with rough locks — it may be a sheep, and *ovis* is a sheep. His sire so strong — a ram is a sheep's sire, that being also an engine of war. Horns he has, and four legs — so has a sheep. Without doubt this monster is a black sheep. Isn't it a sheep that you mean?"

Ovis is Latin for "sheep."

The black sheep's sire is a ram; a battering ram throws down strong walls.

Sir Tophas said, "Thou have hit it; that monster I will kill and sup with."

He will eat the black sheep.

Samias said to his friends, "Come, let us take him off his plan. Let us distract him."

The pages and maidens came forward and said, "Sir Tophas, all hail!"

"Welcome, children," Sir Tophas said. "I seldom cast my eyes as low as to the crowns of your heads, and therefore pardon me that I did not speak all this while."

"No harm done," Dares said. "Here are fair ladies come to marvel at your body, your valor, your wit, the report whereof has made them careless about their own honors, as long as they could glut their eyes and hearts upon yours."

The two young maids-in-waiting were "careless about their own honors" because they were talking to Sir Tophas without chaperones other than the two boy-pages.

Sir Tophas said, "Report and gossip cannot do otherwise than injure me, because, not knowing fully what I am, I fear that gossip has been a niggard in her praises."

Sir Tophas did not know fully what he was: a fool.

Any gossip about him would fail to state just how great a person he really was. So said Sir Tophas.

"No, gentle knight," Scintilla said. "Report has been prodigal, for she has left you no equal, nor herself credit. So much she has told, yet no more than we now see."

Her words were ambiguous. Report of Sir Tophas' reputation had 1) failed to say how great a man he was, or 2) failed to say how outlandish a man he was.

Dares whispered, "She is a good wench."

Favilla said to Sir Tophas, "If there remains in you as much pity toward women as there is in you courage against your enemies, then we women shall be happy, who, hearing about your person, came to see it; and seeing it, are now in love with it."

In love with his body? Or in love with the entertainment that he provides without meaning to?

Sir Tophas said, "Love me, ladies? I easily believe it, but my tough heart receives no impression with sweet words. Mars may pierce it; Venus shall not paint on it."

"That is a cruel saying," Favilla said.

Samias whispered, "There's a girl."

Dares said to Sir Tophas, "Will you cast these ladies away, and all because they want a little love? Do but speak kindly."

Sir Tophas said:

"There comes no soft syllable within my lips. Custom has made my words bloody and my heart barbarous. That paltry, pelting word 'love' — how waterish it is in my mouth! It carries no sound. Hate, horror, death are speeches that nourish my spirits.

"I like honey, but I don't care for the bees because they sting. I delight in music, but I don't love to play on the bagpipes. I can vouchsafe to hear the voice of women, but to touch their bodies I disdain as a thing childish and fit for such men as can digest nothing but milk."

"You have a hard heart," Scintilla said. "Shall we die for your love and find no remedy?"

Sir Tophas said, "I have already taken a surfeit of love and women. I have already had too much of them."

"Good master, pity them," Epiton said.

Sir Tophas said:

"Pity them, Epi? No, I do not think that this breast shall be pestered with such a foolish passion.

"What is that which the gentlewoman carries on a chain?"

"Why, it is a squirrel," Epiton said.

Sir Tophas said, "A squirrel? O gods, what things are made for money!"

"Squirrel" was slang for "prostitute."

The pages and maidens spoke confidentially to each other.

"Isn't this gentleman over-wise?" Dares whispered.

"I could stay all day with him if I didn't fear being shent — being scolded," Favilla whispered.

"Isn't it possible to meet him again?" Scintilla whispered.

"Yes, at any time," Dares whispered.

"Then let us hasten home," Favilla whispered.

Scintilla said out loud, "Sir Tophas, may the god of war deal better with you than you do with the god of love."

The god of love is Cupid.

Favilla said, "We may dissemble and hide our love for now; but we cannot digest and endure your indifference to our love. Still, I don't doubt that time will hamper you and help us."

Sir Tophas said:

"I defy time, who has no interest in and no claim on my heart.

"Come, Epi, let me go to the battle with that hideous beast.

"Love is pap, and love has no relish in my taste because it is not terrible."

"Pap" is baby food, and it is a woman's breast.

Sir Tophas and Epiton exited.

Dares said:

"Indeed, a black sheep is a perilous beast.

"But let us go in until we meet him another time."

Favilla said, "I shall long for that time."

Everyone exited.

Endymion stood near a riverbank on which lunary — moonwort, a species of fern — grew. Unseen by him, Dipsas and Bagoa stood nearby. Bagoa was a sorceress and an assistant to Dipsas.

Endymion said to himself:

"No rest, Endymion? Still uncertain how to settle thy steps by day or thy thoughts by night? Thy truth is measured by thy fortune, and thou are judged unfaithful because thou are unhappy."

Endymion loved Cynthia and he was faithful to her, but she did not love him back, and his fortune was unfortunate and unhappy. Anyone who believed that true love will always be rewarded would regard him as not being truly in love with Cynthia.

Endymion continued:

"I will see if I can beguile myself with sleep, and if no slumber will take hold in my eyes, yet I will embrace the golden thoughts in my head and wish to melt by musing, that as ebony, which no fire can scorch, is yet consumed with sweet savors, so my heart, which cannot be bent by the hardness of fortune, may be bruised by amorous desires."

A false belief about ebony held that when it burned, it had no flame, but it did produce a sweet scent.

Endymion continued:

"On yonder riverbank never grew anything but lunary, and hereafter I will never have any bed but that riverbank.

"O Endymion, Tellus was fair! But what avails beauty without wisdom?

"Nay, Endymion, she was wise. But what avails wisdom without honor?

"She was honorable, Endymion. Don't belie her. Aye, but how obscure is honor without fortune?

"Wasn't she fortunate whom so many followed? Yes, yes, but fortune is base without majesty.

"Thy majesty, Cynthia, all the world knows and wonders at, but not one in the world can imitate it or comprehend it.

"No more, Endymion. Sleep or die. Nay, die, for it is impossible to sleep; and yet (I don't know how it comes to pass) I feel such a heaviness both in my eyes and in my heart that I am suddenly benumbed, yes, in every joint. It may be weariness, for when did I rest? It may be deep melancholy, for when did I not sigh? Cynthia, aye, so I say Cynthia!"

He went to the riverbank, lay down, and fell asleep.

Dipsas stepped forward and said:

"Little do thou know, Endymion, when thou shall wake, for, had thou placed thy heart as low in love as thy head lies now in sleep, thou might have commanded Tellus, whom now instead of a mistress thou shall find a tomb."

Tellus is the goddess of the Earth.

Dipsas continued:

"These eyes I must seal up by art, not by nature, these eyes that are to be opened neither by art nor by nature.

"Thou who lay down with golden locks shall not awaken until they have turned to silver hairs; and that chin, on which scarcely appears soft down, shall be filled with bristles as hard as broom straw. Thou shall sleep out thy youth and flowering time and become dry hay before thou know thyself green grass in the prime of thy life, and thou shall find thyself ready by age to step into the grave when thou wake up — thou who was youthful in the court when thou lay down to sleep.

"The malice of Tellus has brought this to pass, which if she could not have entreated me by fair means, she would have commanded by menacing; for from her we gather all our simples to maintain our sorceries."

Simples are medicines consisting of one ingredient, such as a medicinal herb that grows in earth. These herbs, however, can also be used in witchcraft.

Dipsas then said to Bagoa:

"Fan with this hemlock over his face and sing the enchantment for sleep, while I go and finish those ceremonies that are required in our art. Take care that you don't touch his face, for the fan is so seasoned that whoever it touches with a leaf shall immediately die, and over whom the wind of it breaths, he shall sleep forever."

Bagoa said, "Let me alone and leave it to me, I will be careful."

Dipsas exited.

Bagoa fanned Endymion as she sang the enchantment, and Endymion fell more deeply into sleep.

Bagoa then said:

"What hap — what misfortune — had thou, Endymion, to come under the hands of Dipsas?

"O fair Endymion, how it grieves me that thy fair face must be turned to a withered skin and taste the pains of death before it feels the reward of love!

"I fear that Tellus will repent that which the heavens themselves seemed to rue.

"But I hear Dipsas coming. I dare not repine and complain, lest she make me pine and long for Endymion, and she may rock me into such a deep sleep that I shall not awaken even for my marriage."

Dipsas returned and asked, "How do matters stand now? Have you finished?"

"Yes," Bagoa said.

Dipsas said, "Well, then, let us go in, and see that you do not as much as whisper that I did this; for if you do, I will turn thy hairs to adders and all thy teeth in thy head to tongues.

"Come away. Come away."

They exited, leaving Endymion behind, asleep.

A Dumb Show

Music sounded.

Endymion slept on the riverbank.

Three ladies entered. One lady had a knife and a looking glass, and at the instigation of one of the other two ladies, she made motions as if she would stab Endymion as he slept, but the third lady wrung her hands, lamented, wanting always to prevent it and making motions as if she would prevent it, but not daring to do so. At last, the first lady, looking into the mirror, cast down the knife.

The three ladies exited.

An ancient man entered the scene with books with three leaves. He offered the books to Endymion twice. Endymion refused each time. The old man tore two and offered the third to Endymion. The old man stood for a while, and then Endymion offered to take it.

The ancient man exited.

Endymion remained sleeping on the lunary bank, curtained off from view.

CHAPTER 3

— 3.1 —

Cynthia, Tellus, Semele, Eumenides, Corsites, Panelion, and Zontes met together. Corsites was a captain, and Panelion and Zontes were lords at Cynthia's court.

Cynthia asked, "Is the report true that Endymion is stricken into such a dead sleep that nothing can either awaken him or move him?"

Eumenides answered, "The report is too true, madam, and Endymion is as much to be pitied as wondered at."

"It is as good to sleep and do no harm as it is to wake and do no good," Tellus said.

Cynthia said, "Tellus, what makes you be so short and abrupt? The time was that you thought only about Endymion."

"It is an old saying, madam, that a waking dog from far away barks at a sleeping lion," Eumenides said.

"It would be good, Eumenides, that you took a nap with your friend, for your speech begins to be heavy," Semele said.

Of course, Eumenides' friend Endymion was sleeping a very long sleep.

Heavy speech can be serious speech, or speech that is slurred because of drowsiness.

"That would be contrary to your nature, Semele, which has always been accounted light," Eumenides said.

A light woman is a promiscuous woman.

Angry at the exchange of insults, Cynthia said, "What! Have we here before my face these unseemly and malapert, impertinent overthwarts — these exchanges of rude insults in a quarrel? I will tame your tongues and your thoughts, and I will make your speeches answerable to your duties and your thoughts fit for my dignity; or else I will banish you both from my person and from the world."

"I humbly ask your pardon; but such is my unspotted faith to Endymion that whatsoever seems a needle to prick his finger is a dagger to wound my heart," Eumenides said.

Cynthia asked, "If you are so dear to him, how does it happen that you neither go to see him nor search for a remedy for him?"

Eumenides said:

"I have seen him, to my grief, and I sought a cure with despair because I cannot imagine who should restore Endymion, who is the wonder of all men.

"Your Highness, in your hands the entire compass of the Earth is at command (although not in absolute possession)."

The Moon influences all that is within the circumference of the Earth, as shown by the tides.

Eumenides continued:

"You may show yourself worthy of your sex, worthy of your nature, and worthy of your favor and beauty, if you redeem and rescue that honorable Endymion, whose years of age, now ripening, foretell rare virtues and whose unmellowed conceits promise ripe counsel."

According to Eumenides, his friend Endymion, who was still young, nevertheless showed great promise of possessing future rare and splendid virtues. His thoughts, now still unripened, would become wise counsel.

Cynthia said, "I have tested Endymion, and I conceive greater assurance of his age than I could hope of his youth."

Tellus said, "But the right time, madam, makes crooked that tree that will become a cammock, and a young tree that pricks slightly will grow to become a thorn tree; and therefore, he who began without care to settle his life, it is a sign he will end it without amendment and improvement."

In other words, Tellus was saying that early events predicted later events. A young tree that is made to grow crooked can be made into a cane. A tree that pricks slightly when it is young will have full-grown thorns when it is mature. A young man who begins life without taking care to form good habits and without taking care to avoid forming bad habits will probably end his life without making improvements to his life.

A cammock is a crooked piece of wood that can be made into a cane.

Cynthia said:

"Presumptuous girl, I will make thy tongue an example of unrecoverable displeasure.

"Corsites, carry her to the castle in the desert, there to remain and weave."

Corsites asked, "Shall she work stories, or shall she work poetries? Shall she weave historical, nonfiction stories, or shall she weave fictions?"

Cynthia said:

"It does not matter which. Bah, let her weave both, for she shall find in both of them infinite examples of what punishment long tongues have."

Corsites and Tellus exited.

Cynthia continued:

"Eumenides, if any of the soothsayers in Egypt, or the enchanters in Thessaly, or the philosophers in Greece or all the sages of the world can find a remedy to cure Endymion, I will procure it.

"Therefore, dispatch will all speed.

"You, Eumenides, go to Thessaly.

"You, Zontes, go to Greece (because you are acquainted in Athens).

"You, Panelion, go to Egypt, saying that Cynthia sends, and if you will, commands."

"On bowed knee I give thanks, and with wings on my legs I fly to find a remedy," Eumenides said.

"We are ready at Your Highness' command, and we hope to return to your full content," Zontes said.

Cynthia said, "It shall never be said that Cynthia, whose mercy and goodness fills the heavens with joys and the world with marvels, will allow either Endymion or any other person to perish if he may be protected."

Eumenides said, "Your Majesty's words have always been deeds, and your deeds have always been virtues."

In other words: Your Majesty always fulfills your promises in a virtuous manner.

They exited.

Corsites and Tellus talked together.

Corsites said:

"Here is the castle, fair Tellus, in which you must weave until either time ends your days with death or Cynthia ends her displeasure toward you.

"I am sorry that so fair a face should be subject to so hard a fortune, and I am sorry that the flower of beauty, which is honored in courts, should here wither in prison."

Tellus said, "Corsites, Cynthia may restrain the liberty of my body, but she cannot restrain the liberty of my thoughts. And therefore, I esteem myself to be most free, although I am in greatest bondage."

"Can you then feed yourself on fancy, and subdue the malice of envy by the sweetness of imagination?" Corsites asked.

Whose malicious envy? That of Tellus?

Tellus said, "Corsites, there is no sweeter music to the miserable than despair; and therefore, the more bitterness I feel, the more sweetness I find. For so vain was liberty, and so unwelcome was the following of higher fortune, that I choose rather to pine in this castle than to be a prince in any other court."

"That is a humor — an attitude — contrary to your years and not at all agreeable to your sex, the one commonly allured with delights, the other always allured with sovereignty," Corsites said.

Tellus said, "I marvel, Corsites, that you, being a captain, who should sound nothing but terror and suck nothing but blood, can find in your heart to talk such smooth words, because it does not agree with your calling to use words as soft as that of 'love.'"

"Smooth" can mean 1) pleasant and polite, 2) insinuating, or 3) flattering.

Corsites said, "Lady, it would be unfit to discourse with women about wars, as into women's minds nothing can sink but smoothness. Besides, you must not think that soldiers are so rough-hewn or of such knotty metal — knotty material — and knotty mettle that beauty cannot allure, and you, being beyond perfection, enchant."

"Good Corsites, don't talk about love, but let me go to my labor," Tellus said. "The little beauty I have shall be bestowed on my loom, which I now mean to make my lover."

"Let us go in, and what favor Corsites can show, Tellus can command," Corsites said.

"The only favor I desire is now and then to walk," Tellus said.

Sir Tophas, armed, and Epiton, carrying a gown (an outer garment for men) and other paraphernalia, talked together.

"Epi!" Sir Tophas said.

"Here, sir," Epiton said.

"Unrig me," Sir Tophas said. "Heighho!"

"What's that?" Epiton asked.

He was asking about "heighho."

Sir Tophas answered, "An interjection, whereof some are of mourning, such as *eho, yah*."

Instead of *eho*, aka "holla," Sir Tophas may have meant *eheu*, aka "alas."

These words are interjections from a Latin grammar book of the time. The book was written by William Lyly, John Lyly's grandfather.

"I don't understand you," Epiton said.

Sir Tophas asked, "Do thou see me?"

"Aye," Epiton said.

Sir Tophas asked, "Do thou hear me?"

"Aye," Epiton said.

Sir Tophas asked, "Do thou feel me?"

"Aye," Epiton said.

Sir Tophas asked, "And do thou understand me?"

"No," Epiton said.

Sir Tophas said:

"Then I am but three quarters of a noun substantive."

According to William Lyly's Latin grammar book, a noun substantive can be seen, heard, felt, and understood.

Sir Tophas then said:

"But alas, Epi, to tell thee the truth, I am a noun adjective."

According to William Lyly's Latin grammar book, a noun adjective cannot stand by itself. It needs another word to support it. Today, we call noun adjectives simply adjectives.

"Why?" Epiton asked.

Sir Tophas said, "Because I cannot stand without another."

One meaning of "stand" is "to have an erection."

"Who is that?" Epiton asked. "Who is 'another'?"

Sir Tophas said, "Dipsas."

"Are you in love?" Epiton asked.

Sir Tophas said:

"No, but love has, as it were, milked my thoughts and drained from my heart the very substance of my accustomed courage."

In this society, people believed that each sigh drained away a drop of blood from the heart.

Sir Tophas continued:

"It works and ferments in my head like new wine, and so I must hoop my sconce with iron lest my head break and I betray and reveal my brains."

A sconce is 1) a small fortress, or 2) a head.

The word that John Lyly used for "betray" is "bewray," which sounds like "beray," which means to soil oneself.

Sir Tobias continued:

"But please, first reveal and expose me in all parts, so that I may be like a lover, and then I will sigh and die. Take my gun and give me a gown. *Cedant arma togae* — let arms yield to the toga."

In other words: Let the weapons of war yield to diplomacy.

Epiton helped Sir Tophas to disarm and then gave him the gown, saying, "Here."

Sir Tophas said, "Take my sword and shield and give me a beard-brush and scissors. *Bella gerant alii; tu, Pari, semper ama* — let others fight; you, Paris, will always love."

If Sir Tophas is to be compared to the Trojan prince Paris, then his beloved, the aged sorceress Dipsas, whose nose touches her chin, is to be compared to Helen of Troy, the most beautiful woman in the world.

"Will you be trimmed, sir?" Epiton asked.

Sir Tophas said:

"Not yet, for I feel a contention within me whether I shall frame the bodkin beard or the bush."

The bodkin beard was shaped like a dagger, and the bush beard was bushy.

Later, we learn that three or four little hairs are growing on Sir Tophas' chin.

Sir Tophas then said:

"But take my pike and give me a pen. *Dicere quae puduit, scribere jussit amor* — love makes one write about things he cannot speak about."

"I will furnish and equip you, sir," Epiton said.

Sir Tophas said:

"Now for my bow and bolts, give me ink and paper; and for my smiter, give me a penknife."

"Bolts" are arrows.

Sir Tophas continued:

"For *scalpellum, calami, atramentum, charta, libelli, sint semper studiis arma parata meis* — may penknife, pens, ink, papers, books always be prepared for action."

"Sir, will you give over wars and play with that bauble — that plaything — called love?" Epiton asked.

Sir Tophas said:

"Give over wars? Give them up? No, Epi.

"*Militat omnis amans, et habet sua castra Cupido* — all lovers are warriors, and Cupid has his own military camp."

"Love has made you very eloquent, but your face is not at all fair and handsome," Epiton said.

Sir Tophas said, "*Non formosus erat, sed erat facundus Ulysses* — Ulysses was not handsome, but he was eloquent."

"Nay, I must seek a new master if you can speak nothing but verses," Epiton said.

Sir Tophas said:

"*Quicquid conabar dicere versus erat* — what I was trying to speak were verses.

"Epi, I feel all Ovid's *De Arte Amandi* lie as heavy at my heart as a load of logs."

Ovid wrote *Ars Amatoria*: *The Art of Love*. It was also known as *De Arte Amandi*.

Sir Tophas continued:

"O what a fine thin hair has Dipsas!

"What a pretty low forehead!"

"Thin hair" can mean "balding."

This society praised high foreheads.

Sir Tophas continued:

"What a tall and stately nose!

"What little hollow eyes!

"What great and goodly lips!

"How harmless she is, being toothless!

"Her fingers are fat and short, and they are adorned with long nails like a bittern — like a heron with long claws!

"In how sweet a proportion her cheeks hang down to her breasts like dugs [udders] and her paps [her breasts] hang down to her waist like bags!

"What a low stature she is, and yet what a great big foot she carries!

"How thrifty must she be in whom there is no waste!"

And no waist.

Sir Tophas continued:

"How virtuous she is likely to be, about whom no man can be jealous!"

"Stop, master, you forget yourself," Epiton said.

Sir Tophas said, "O, Epi, even as a dish melts by the fire, so does my wit increase by love."

His comparison lacks wit and intelligence.

"Pithily, and to the purpose," Epiton said sarcastically about Sir Tophas' choice of a metaphor. "But what now? Do you begin to nod?"

Sir Tophas said, "Good Epi, let me take a nap. For as some man may better steal a horse than another man may look over the hedge, so many different people shall be sleepy when they would most like to take a rest."

He slept.

Epiton said to himself:

"Who ever saw such a woodcock?"

A woodcock is an easily caught bird, and so "a woodcock" became slang for "a fool."

Epiton continued:

"Love Dipsas? Without doubt all the world will now account him valiant, him who ventures on her whom no one dared to undertake.

"But here come two wags."

Samias and Dares entered the scene.

Samias said to Dares, "Thy master has slept his share."

Dares was the sleeping Endymion's page.

Dares said to Samias, "I think he does it because he doesn't want to pay me my board wages: my allowance to buy food."

Samias said, "It is a very strange thing, and I think my master will never return; so that we must both seek new masters, for we shall never live by our manners."

Samias was Eumenides' page; Eumenides had gone to Thessaly to seek a cure for the sleeping Endymion.

Epiton said to Samias and Dares, "If you want manners, join with me and serve Sir Tophas, who must keep more men because he is heading toward marriage."

"Want" can mean 1) lack, and 2) desire.

"What, Epi? Where's thy master?" Samias asked.

"Yonder sleeping in love," Epiton answered.

"Is it possible?" Dares asked.

He did not expect Sir Tophas to be in love.

Epiton said, "He has taken his thoughts a hole lower, aka down a peg, and he has come off his high horse, and he says, seeing it is the fashion of the world, he will vail bonnet — take off his hat — to beauty."

"A hole lower." Hmm. Women have a hole lower.

A ship that surrenders will vail — lower — its sails.

"How is he attired?" Samias asked.

"Lovely — like a lover," Epiton answered.

"Whom does this amorous knight love?" Dares asked.

"Dipsas," Epiton answered.

"That ugly creature?" Samias said. "Why, she is a fool, a scold, fat, without fashion and shape, and quite without favor and beauty."

"Tush, you are simple-minded," Epiton said. "My master has a good marriage in mind."

"Good?" Dares said. "In what way?"

Epiton said:

"Why, in marrying Dipsas, he shall have every day twelve dishes of food for his dinner, although there will be none but Dipsas with him.

"Four dishes of flesh, four dishes of fish, four dishes of fruit."

"How, Epi?" Samias asked.

Epiton said, "For flesh, these: woodcock, goose, bittern, and rail."

"Woodcock" and "goose" mean "fool."

Bittens are a species of bird that has long claws. Dipsas will scratch Sir Tophas.

Rails are crane-like birds, but the name suggests that Dipsas will rail at and criticize Sir Tophas.

"Indeed, he shall not miss having those if Dipsas is there," Dares said.

Epiton said, "For fish, these are the dishes: crab, carp, lump, and pouting."

"Excellent!" Samias said. "For, of my word, she is crabbish, lumpish, and carping."

And pouting.

All of these fish dishes, including lump and pouting, are real fish.

Epiton said:

"For fruit these are the dishes: fritters, medlars, heart-i-chokes, and lady-longings."

Three of the fruits are varieties of apples.

Dipsas is a fretting woman.

Medlars were eaten when they were soft and beginning to rot. Dipsas was a meddling woman, and she was an aging woman who was beginning to rot.

"Heart-i-chokes" are, of course, artichokes. Dipsas can choke a heart.

"Lady-longings" refers to a woman's desires.

Epiton then said:

"Thus, you see he shall fare like a king, although he is only a beggar."

Dares said:

"Well, Epi, dine thou with him, for I had rather fast than see her face.

"But see, thy master is asleep. Let us have a song to wake this amorous knight."

"Agreed," Epiton said.

"I am content to sing," Samias said.

They began to sing their song.

Epiton sang:

"Here snores Sir Tophas,

"That amorous ass,

"Who loves Dipsas,

"With face so sweet.

"Nose and chin meet."

All three sang:

"At sight of her each Fury skips

"And flings into her lap their whips."

Furies are whip-carrying avenging deities from the Land of the Dead.

Dares sang:

"Holla, holla in his ear."

Samias sang:

"The witch sure [surely] thrust her fingers there."

Epiton sang:

"Cramp him, or wring the fool by the nose."

Wringing an unconscious person's nose was supposed to restore that person to consciousness.

These three servants would also be happy to give Sir Tophas cramps — or to burn his toes.

Dares sang:

"Or clap some burning flax to his toes."

Samias sang:

"What music's best to wake him?"

Epiton sang:

"Bow-wow. Let bandogs shake him."

Bandogs are tied-up fierce dogs.

Dares sang:

"Let adders hiss in his ear."

Samias sang:

"Else earwigs wriggle there."

Earwigs are a species of crawling insects.

Epiton sang:

"No, let him batten; when his tongue

"Once goes, a cat is not worse strung."

Cat guts were used as strings in musical instruments.

To "batten" means to "grow fat."

All three sang:

"But if he ope nor [opens neither] mouth nor eyes,

"He may in time sleep himself wise."

Sir Tophas said to himself, as he awakened, "Sleep is a binding of the senses; love is a loosing of the senses."

Epiton whispered to Samias and Dares, "Let us listen to him for a while."

Sir Tophas said, "There appeared in my sleep a goodly owl, who, sitting on my shoulder, cried, 'Twit, twit,' and in front of my eyes presented herself as the express image of Dipsas. I marveled at what the owl said, until at the last I perceived 'Twit, twit' to mean 'To it, to it.' Only by contraction was I admonished by this vision to make account of my sweet Venus."

Another interpretation of the dream is that the owl was simply making its cry — not telling him to "go to it" and woo Dipsas.

In this society, a twit is a criticism or a reproach.

Samias said, "Sir Tophas, you have overslept yourself."

Sir Tophas replied, "No, youth, I have but slept over my love."

"Slept over my love"? Hmm. Slept on top of my love?

Dares said, "Love? Why, it is impossible that into so noble and unconquered a courage, love should creep, having first a head as hard to pierce as steel, and then to pass to a heart armed with a shirt of mail — that is, with armor."

A "head as hard to pierce as steel" is one armed with a helmet against an enemy, or one armed with stupidity against ideas.

Epiton whispered to Samias and Dares, "Aye, but my master yawning one day in the sun, love crept into his mouth before he could close it, and there kept such a tumbling in his body that he was glad to untruss the points — to untie the strings — of his heart and entertain and welcome Love as a stranger."

Sir Tophas said, "If there remains any pity in you, plead for me to Dipsas."

"Plead?" Dares said. "Nay, we will press her to it."

Dares whispered to Samias:

"Let us go with him to Dipsas, and there we shall have good sport — good entertainment."

He then said out loud:

"But Sir Tophas, when shall we go? For I find my tongue voluble and my heart venturous, and I find all myself like myself."

Samias whispered, "Come, Dares, let us not lose him until we find our masters, for as long as he lives, we shall lack neither mirth nor meat."

Epiton said:

"We will traverse. We will proceed."

He then asked Sir Tophas:

"Will you go, sir?"

Sir Tophas said, "Will I go? *Prae, sequar* — lead, I will follow."

They exited to go and see Dipsas.

— 3.4 —

Eumenides and Geron met outside, near a fountain.

Geron, an old man, sang a sad song.

Eumenides would call Geron "father," a respectful way of addressing an old man, even when the old man was not one's biological father.

Eumenides said, "Father, your sad and solemn music, being tuned to the same key that my hard fortune is, has so melted my mind that I wish to hang at your mouth's end until my life ends."

Geron said, "These tunes, gentleman, I have been accustomed to sing these fifty winters, having no other house to shroud myself but the broad heavens; and continual experience has made misery so familiar to me that I esteem sorrow my chiefest solace. And most welcome is that guest who can rehearse — can relate — the saddest tale or the bloodiest tragedy to me."

"This is a strange humor — a strange disposition," Eumenides said. "Might I inquire its cause?"

Geron said:

"You must pardon me if I decline to tell it, for, knowing that the revealing of griefs is, as it were, a renewing of sorrow, I have vowed therefore to conceal them so that I might not only feel the depth of everlasting discontentment, but also despair of remedy.

"But from where are you? What fortune has thrust you into this distress?"

Eumenides said, "I am going to Thessaly to seek remedy for Endymion, my dearest friend, who has been cast into a dead sleep almost these twenty years, growing old and ready for the grave, being almost but newly come forth from the cradle."

"You need not travail and travel far for a remedy because the person who can clearly see the bottom of this fountain shall have the remedy for any problem," Geron said.

"That, I think, is impossible," Eumenides said. "Why, what virtue can there be in water?"

"Yes, whoever can shed the tears of a faithful lover into the fountain shall obtain anything he wishes," Geron said. "Read these words engraved around the brim."

Eumenides read words that backed up what Geron had said, and then he said, "Have you known this by experience? Have you witnessed this happening? Will the tears of a faithful lover be in fact rewarded? Or was this fountain placed here on purpose to delude men?"

Geron said, "I would only like to have experience of it, myself, and then there would be an end of my misery. And then I would tell you the strangest discourse that ever yet was heard."

Eumenides said to himself, but loudly enough for Geron to hear, "Ah, Eumenides!"

He had two problems. One, he loved Semele, but she did not return his love, and so he needed a remedy that would result in her loving him. Two, he loved Endymion as a friend, and he needed a remedy to awaken him from his too-deep sleep.

Which wish did he most want fulfilled?

"What do you need, gentleman?" Geron asked. "Aren't you well?"

"Yes, father, but a qualm that often comes over my heart now takes hold of me," Eumenides said. "But have any lovers ever come hither?"

Geron said:

"Lusters have come here, but not lovers."

Lusters are those who lust. Lusters are also appearances.

Geron continued:

"For often I have seen them weep, but I could never hear that they saw the bottom."

"Have women come there, also?" Eumenides asked.

"Some," Geron said.

"What did they see?" Eumenides asked.

Geron answered, "They all wept with the result that the fountain overflowed with tears, but so thick became the water with their tears that I could scarcely discern the brim, much less behold the bottom."

"Are faithful lovers so scant?" Eumenides asked.

"It seems so, for I have never heard of any yet," Geron said.

Eumenides said to himself, but loudly enough for Geron to hear:

"Ah, Eumenides, how are thou perplexed!

"Call to mind the beauty of thy sweet mistress and the depth of thy never-dying affections. How often have thou honored her, not only without spot — without sin — but also without suspicion of falsehood! And how hardly has she rewarded thee without cause or reason or color of despite — without pretext for her scorn of me! How secret have thou been these seven years, who have not named her — who have not even once dared to name her for fear of discontenting her.

"Unhappy Eumenides!"

"Why, gentleman, did you once love?" Geron asked.

"Once?" Eumenides said. "Aye, father, and I always shall."

"Was she unkind and were you faithful?" Geron asked.

"She is of all women the most froward, the most perverse, and I am of all creatures the fondest, the most foolish," Eumenides said.

"You doted then, not loved," Geron said. "For affection is grounded on virtue and virtue is never peevish, or affection is based on beauty, and beauty loves to be praised."

Both virtue and beauty can be loved. And praised.

According to Geron's words, because Semele was peevish, Eumenides could not truly love her — he could only dote on her. But Semele was beautiful.

Eumenides said, "Aye, but if all virtuous ladies should yield to all who are loving, or if all amiable gentlewomen should entertain all who are amorous, their virtues would be accounted vices and their beauties would be accounted deformities, because love can be only between two, and that not proceeding from him who is most faithful, but from him who is most fortunate."

A woman does not always fall in love with the man who most loves her.

"I wish that you were so faithful that your tears might make you fortunate," Geron said.

"Yes, father, if it is the case that my tears do not clear this fountain, then you may swear that the fountain is only a mere mockery," Eumenides said.

"So, indeed, everyone yet who wept," Geron said.

In other words: Every lover — make that luster — who has wept into the fountain has not been able to see the fountain's bottom, and so the fountain has shown that the lusters' love is not true. Like Eumenides would do if he could not see the fountain's bottom, they had said that the fountain was a mere mockery.

Looking into the fountain, Eumenides said, "Ah, I faint, I die! Ah, sweet Semele, let me alone and leave it to me, and let me dissolve by weeping into water!"

Geron said to himself, "This affection seems strange. It may be affectation. If he sees nothing, without doubt this dissembling is excessive, for nothing shall draw me away from the belief that the fountain has magical properties."

Eumenides said, "Father, I plainly see the bottom, and there in white marble are engraved these words: 'Ask one for all, and ask for only one thing at all.'"

The words mean, "Ask for just one remedy out of all of those that you might ask for."

Geron said:

"O fortunate Eumenides (for so I have heard thee call thyself), let me see."

He looked into the fountain, and then he said:

"I cannot discern any such thing. I think thou dream."

Eumenides said, "Ah, father, thou are not a faithful lover and therefore cannot behold it."

"Then ask, so that I may be satisfied by the outcome, and thyself blessed," Geron said.

Eumenides said:

"Ask? So I will. And what shall I do but ask, and whom should I ask for but Semele, the possessing of whose person is a pleasure that cannot come within the compass of comparison, whose golden locks seem most artfully arranged when they seem most carelessly arranged, whose sweet looks seem most alluring when they are most chaste, and whose words the more virtuous they are, the more amorous they are accounted.

"I pray to thee, Fortune, when I shall first meet with fair Semele, dash my delight with some light disgrace lest embracing sweetness beyond measure, I take surfeit without a remedy.

"Let her practice her accustomed coyness, so that I may diet myself upon my desires; otherwise, the fullness of my joys will diminish the sweetness, and I shall perish by them before I possess them."

He was worried that the pleasure of Semele's loving him could destroy him.

In mythology, a mortal woman named Semele had sex with Jupiter, King of the gods, after making him swear an inviolable oath that he would grant her whatever she wished for. After they had sex, Semele asked Jupiter to reveal himself to her in his true form. Having sworn an inviolable oath, Jupiter had to grant the wish, but seeing Jupiter in his true form was too much for Semele, and she died. She was carrying a fetus, which Jupiter rescued and sewed into his thigh. Jupiter later gave birth to Bacchus, the god of wine and ecstasy.

Eumenides continued:

"Why do I trifle away the time in words? The least minute being spent in the getting of Semele is worth more than the whole world; therefore, let me ask for Semele.

"What now, Eumenides? To where are thou drawn? Have thou forgotten both friendship and duty, both the care of Endymion and the commandment of Cynthia? Shall he die in a leaden sleep because thou sleep in a golden dream?

"Aye, let him sleep always, as long as I slumber just one minute with Semele. Love knows neither friendship nor kindred. Why wouldn't I hazard the loss of a friend, for the obtaining of her for whom I would often lose myself?

"Fond and foolish Eumenides, shall the enticing beauty of a most disdainful lady be of more force than the rare fidelity of a tried friend? The love of men to women is a thing that is common and of a matter-of-fact course; the friendship of man to man is infinite, and it is immortal.

"Tush, Semele possesses my love.

"Aye, but Endymion has deserved it. I will help Endymion; I found Endymion unspotted in his truth.

"Aye, but I shall find Semele constant in her love. I will have Semele.

"What shall I do? Father, thy gray hairs are ambassadors of experience. Which shall I ask?"

He had to choose between Semele and Endymion. One was a woman whom he loved, and the other was a friend.

Geron advised:

"Eumenides, release Endymion; for all things, friendship excepted, are subject to fortune. Love is just an eye-worm — a distraction, a woman whom one eyes — which only tickles the head with hopes and wishes; friendship is the image of eternity, in which there is nothing movable, nothing mischievous.

"As much difference as there is between beauty and virtue, bodies and shadows, colors [makeup] and life, so great differences are there between love and friendship. Love is a chameleon, which draws nothing into the mouth but air and nourishes nothing in the body but lungs."

A folk belief in this society was that chameleons can live on nothing but air.

Geron continued:

"Believe me, Eumenides, desire dies in the same moment that beauty sickens, and beauty fades in the same instant that it flourishes. When adversities flow, then love ebbs, but friendship stands stiffly in storms. Time draws wrinkles in a fair face but adds fresh colors to a fast friend, which neither heat, nor cold, nor misery, nor place, nor destiny can alter or diminish.

"O friendship, of all things the most rare and uncommon, and therefore the rarest and most splendid because the most excellent, whose comforts in misery are always sweet and whose counsels in prosperity are always fortunate!

"Vain love, which only comes near to friendship in name, wishes to seem to be the same, or better, in nature!"

Amor is Latin for "love," and *amicitia* is Latin for "friendship." Geron valued friendship much more than he valued love, and he criticized love as being vain for trading on the similarity of *amor* to *amicitia* and claiming to be superior to *amicitia*.

Eumenides said:

"Father, I allow your reasons and will therefore conquer my own. Virtue shall subdue affections, wisdom shall subdue lust, friendship shall subdue beauty. Mistresses are in every place, and as common as hares on Mount Athos, bees in the Sicilian city of Hybla (which is famous for its honey), fowls in the air; but friends to be found are like the phoenix in Arabia, just one, or the *philadelphi* in Arays, never more than two. I will have Endymion."

Mount Athos is the site of many Eastern Orthodox monasteries. The monks have full beards, and so, yes, there are many hairs on Mount Athos.

The phoenix was a mythological Arabian bird that lived for five hundred years, burned itself up, and rose reborn from the ashes.

"*Philadelphi* in Arays" may mean *philadelphi ad aras*, a variant of the proverb "friendship as far as the altar," or "friendship to the point of conscience." If this is the case, then the proverb puts friendship before all things except God, Who comes first and Who is all-good and Who wants us to follow our conscience.

Or *philadelphi* could mean *philadelphus hirsutus*, or mock-orange, whose flowers grow in twos.

The Greek *philadelphus* means "loving one's sibling," and so *philadelphi* may refer to loving brothers and to brotherly love.

Arays could be a place: the Spanish Araya or Aranjuez, whose old Latin name is *Ara Iovis*.

Eumenides looked into the fountain again and said:

"Sacred fountain, in whose bowels are hidden divine secrets, I have increased your waters with the tears of unspotted thoughts, and therefore let me receive the reward you promise. Endymion, the truest friend to me, and the most faithful lover to Cynthia, is in such a dead sleep that nothing can wake or move him."

"Do thou see anything?" Geron asked.

Eumenides said:

"I see in the same white marble pillar these words: 'When she, whose figure of all is the most perfect and never to be measured, always one yet never the same, always inconstant yet never wavering, shall come and kiss Endymion in his sleep, he shall then rise; else he will never rise.'

"This is strange."

"What else do you see?" Geron asked.

Endymion said, "There comes over my eyes either a dark mist, or upon the fountain a deep thickness, for I can perceive nothing. But how I am deluded! Or what difficult, nay impossible, thing is this?"

"I think it is easy to understand," Geron said.

"Good father, and how?" Eumenides asked.

"Isn't a circle of all figures the most perfect?" Geron asked.

"Yes," Eumenides said.

"And isn't Cynthia of all circles the most absolute?" Geron asked.

The full Moon is round.

"Yes," Eumenides said.

"Isn't it impossible to measure her, who always works by her influence, never standing at one stay?" Geron asked.

According to astrologers, heavenly bodies such as the Moon influenced human destiny.

"One stay" is one fixed place in the zodiac. The Moon, of course, varies its position in the night sky.

"Yes," Eumenides said.

Geron said, "Isn't she always Cynthia, yet seldom in the same bigness, always wavering in her waxing or waning, so that our bodies might the better be governed, our seasons the daylier give their increase, yet never to be removed from her course as long as the heavens continue theirs?"

The Moon each day increases the seasons, which go from one to another.

"Yes," Eumenides said.

Geron said, "Then who can it be but Cynthia, whose virtues being all divine, must necessarily bring things to pass that are miraculous? Go humble thyself to Cynthia; tell her the success, aka the outcome of your quest, of which I myself shall be a witness. And assure thyself of this: that she who sent thee to find the means for Endymion's safety will now work her cunning skill."

"How fortunate I am, if Cynthia is she who may do it!" Eumenides said.

Geron said, "How fond — how foolish — thou are if you do not believe it!"

"I will hasten thither, so that I may entreat on my knees for succor, and I will embrace in my arms my friend," Eumenides said.

"I will go with thee, for to Cynthia I must reveal all my sorrows, who also must work in me a contentment," Geron said.

"May I now know the cause?" Eumenides asked.

"That shall be my tale as we walk, and I don't doubt that the strangeness of my tale will take away the tediousness of our journey," Geron said.

"Let us go," Eumenides said.

"I follow," Geron said.

They exited.

CHAPTER 4

— 4.1 —

Alone, Tellus said to herself:

"I marvel that Corsites gives me so much liberty, with all the world knowing his charge and commission to be so high and of such magnitude and his nature to be most strange and reserved. He has so badly treated ladies of great honor in that he has not allowed them to look out of windows, much less to walk abroad.

"It may be the case that he is in love with me, for, Endymion, hardhearted Endymion excepted, who is he who is not enamored of my beauty?

"But what respect do thou, Tellus, give the love of all the world? Endymion hates thee. Alas, poor Endymion, my malice has exceeded my love, and thy faith and loyalty to Cynthia has quenched my affections.

"Quenched, Tellus? Nay, kindled them afresh, insomuch that I find scorching flames instead of dead embers, and cruel encounters of war in my thoughts instead of sweet parleys.

"Ah, that I might once again see Endymion! Accursed girl, what hope have thou to see Endymion, on whose head already are grown gray hairs, and whose life must yield to nature before Cynthia shall end her displeasure?

"Wicked Dipsas, and most devilish Tellus, the one — Dipsas — for cunning too exquisite, and the other — Tellus — for hate too intolerable!

"Thou, Tellus, were commanded to weave the stories and poetries wherein were shown both examples and punishments of tattling tongues, and thou have only embroidered the sweet face of Endymion, devices of love, melancholy imaginations, and what not out of thy work — all things that thou should work to pick out of thy mind."

Tellus should have been trying to get Endymion out of her mind.

Tellus continued:

"But here comes Corsites. I must seem yielding and stout, full of mildness yet tempered with a majesty."

"Stout" means "unyielding." She needed to find a mean between extremes.

Tellus continued:

"For if I am too flexible, I shall give him more hope than I mean; and if I am too froward and perverse, I shall enjoy less liberty than I wish to enjoy. I cannot love him, and therefore I will practice that which is most 'contrary' to our sex: to dissemble."

Many people in this society would say without irony that to dissemble is most customary to the female sex.

Corsites entered the scene.

"Fair Tellus," he said, "I perceive that you rise with the lark and that you sing with the nightingale to yourself."

"My lord, I have no playfellow except fancy and my imagination," Tellus said. "Being barred of all company, I must question — converse — with myself and make my thoughts my friends."

Corsites replied, "I wish that you would consider my thoughts to be also your friends, for they are such as are only busied in marveling at your beauty and wisdom, and some of my thoughts are such as have esteemed your fortune too hard, and other thoughts of that kind that offer to set you free if you will set them free."

Tellus said, "There are no colors as contrary as white and black, nor elements as disagreeing as fire and water, nor anything as opposite as men's thoughts and their words."

"Colors" can mean pretenses as well as hues.

Corsites said, "He who gave Cassandra the gift of prophesying, with the curse that, although she spoke so true, she should never be believed, has, I think, poisoned the fortune of men, who, uttering the extremities of their inward passions, are always suspected of outward perjuries."

The god Apollo promised to give the Trojan princess Cassandra the gift of prophecy if she slept with him. She agreed, he gave her the gift, and then she did not keep her promise to sleep with him. Apollo arranged things so that although Cassandra always accurately foretold the future, no one ever believed what she foretold until it happened.

Corsites was saying that Apollo had arranged things so that no matter how truly men spoke about love, women would never believe them.

"Well, Corsites, I will flatter myself and believe you," Tellus said. "What would you do to enjoy my love?"

"I would set all the ladies of the castle free and make you the pleasure of my life," Corsites said. "More I cannot do; less I will not do."

"These are great words, and fit for your calling, for captains must promise impossible things," Tellus said. "But will you do one thing for all?"

"Anything, sweet Tellus," Corsites said. "I am ready to do anything for you."

"You know that on the lunary bank Endymion is sleeping," Tellus said.

"I know it," Corsites said.

Tellus said, "If you will remove him from that place by force and convey him into some obscure cave through cunning, I give you here the faith of an unspotted virgin that only you shall possess me as a lover and, in spite of malicious gossip, have me for a wife."

"Remove him from that place, Tellus?" Corsites said. "Yes, Tellus, he shall be removed, and that so quickly that thou shall as much commend my diligence as my force. I go."

He started to leave.

"Wait," Tellus said. "Will you yourself attempt to remove him?"

Corsites said:

"Aye, Tellus. As I would have no one be partaker of my sweet love, so no one shall be a partner in my labors.

"But I ask thee to go into the castle at your best leisure, for Cynthia begins to rise, and if she discovers our love, we will both perish, for nothing pleases her but the fairness of virginity. All things must be not only without lust but without suspicion of lightness and wantonness."

"I will depart, and you will go to Endymion," Tellus said.

"I fly, Tellus, being of all men the most fortunate," Corsites said.

He exited.

Tellus said:

"Simple Corsites! I have set thee to do a task, thou who are just a man, that the gods themselves cannot perform. For little do thou know how heavy his head lies, how hard his fortune. But women must have such shifts and tricks to deceive men, and, under color — under the pretext — of easy things, entreat that which is impossible. Otherwise, we would be encumbered with importunities, oaths, sighs, letters, and all implements of love, which to one resolved to the contrary, are most loathsome.

"I will go in and laugh with the other ladies at Corsites' sweating."

She exited.

Samias and Dares talked together.

"Will thy master never awake?" Samias asked.

"No, I think he sleeps for a wager," Dares answered. "But how shall we spend the time? Sir Tophas is so far in love that he pines in his bed and does not come abroad."

The pages could not laugh at Sir Tophas because he no longer went outside.

"But here comes Epi, in a pelting chafe: a childish bad mood," Samias said.

Epiton entered the scene.

He said, "A pox on all false proverbs! And, if a proverb were a page, I would have him by the ears."

"Why are thou angry?" Samias asked.

"Why?" Epiton said. "You know that it is said that the tide tarries no man."

Actually, the proverb is, "The tide waits for no man," and not, "The tide delays no man."

Epiton would have been correct if he had said, "The tide tarries *for* no man."

"True," Samias said.

"That is a monstrous lie," Epiton said, "for I was tied two hours, and tarried for one to unloose me."

"Alas, poor Epi!" Dares said.

He meant that Epiton ought to be pitied.

"Poor?" Epiton said. "No, no, you base-conceited slaves, I am a most complete gentleman, although I am in disgrace with Sir Tophas."

Epiton was taking "poor" in the senses of 1) impoverished, and 2) poor-spirited.

"Are thou out of favor with him?" Dares asked.

"Aye, because I cannot get him a lodging with Endymion," Epiton said. "Sir Tophas would like to take a nap for forty or fifty years."

Endymion was in love, and he was sleeping a very long time, Sir Tophas was in love, and he wanted to do as lovers do, and so he wanted to imitate Endymion.

"A 'short' sleep, considering our long life," Dares said.

He was sarcastic.

"Is Sir Tophas still in love?" Samias asked.

"In love?" Epiton said. "Why, he does nothing but make sonnets."

"Can thou remember any one of his poems?" Samias asked.

Epiton said:

"Aye, this is one:

"*The beggar Love that knows not where to lodge,*

"*At last within my heart when I slept,*

"*He crept.*

"*I waked, and so my fancies began to fodge.*'"

"To fodge" means "to proceed."

"That's a very long verse," Samias said. He was referring to this line:

"*I waked, and so my fancies began to fodge.*"

That line was eleven syllables long.

Epiton said:

"Why, the other was short."

The line "*At last within my heart when I slept,*" is nine syllables long.

The lines of Sir Tophas' poem vary in length.

Elizabethan sonnets have fourteen lines and are written in iambic pentameter, and so they have ten syllables per line.

Epiton continued:

"The first is called from the thumb to the little finger, the second from the little finger to the elbow, and some he has made to reach to the crown of his head and down again to the sole of his foot.

He was pretending to literally measure the length of Sir Tophas' lines.

Poetic feet are repeating lines of syllables that are either stressed or unstressed in a certain pattern. For example, an iambic foot consists of two syllables: The first is unstressed and the second is stressed. An iambic pentameter line consists of five iambic feet. For example, this iambic pentameter line comes from William Shakespeare's *Romeo and Juliet*: "*Two households, both alike in dignity.*"

Epiton continued:

"It is set to the tune of the 'Black Saunce'; *ratio est* — the reason is — because Dipsas is a black saint."

"Black Saunce" is "Black Sanctus," a parodic hymn to Satan; it mocked monks.

As a sorceress, Dipsas is the opposite of a saint and so she is a black saint.

Dares said:

"Very wisely.

"But please, Epi, how are thou complete — how are you getting what you need? And, being away from thy master, what occupation will thou take?"

Epiton had said he was a complete gentleman, but to be complete, a person needs to have what is necessary. Epiton had no job, so how could he get what he needed?

Epiton said:

"Know, my hearts, I am an absolute microcosmos, a petty world unto myself. My library is my head, for I have no other books but my brains; my wardrobe is on my back, for I have no more apparel than is on my body; my armory at my fingers' ends, for I use no other artillery than my fingernails; my treasure is in my purse.

"*Sic omnia mea mecum porto* — thus, I carry with me everything that is mine."

"Good," Dares said.

Epiton said, "Now, sirs, my palace is paved with grass and tiled with stars, for *caelo tegitur qui non habet urnam*: He who has no house must lie in the yard."

The Latin sentence actually means this: "He who has no burial urn has the heavens for a roof."

"A brave resolution," Samias said. "But how will thou spend thy time?"

"Not in any melancholy sort. For my exercise I will walk horses," Epiton said.

"Too bad," Dares said.

"Why, isn't it said, 'It is good walking when one has his horse in his hand'?" Epiton asked.

Yes, but Epiton would not be walking his own horse.

"Worse and worse," Samias said. "But how will thou live?

"By angling," Epiton said. "O, it is a stately occupation to stand four hours in a cold morning and to have his nose bitten with frost before his bait is mumbled by a fish."

"To mumble" means "to chew without teeth."

"A rare attempt," Dares said. "But will thou never travel?"

"Yes, in a western barge, when, with a good wind and lusty pugs, one may go ten miles in two days," Epiton said.

"Lusty pugs" are "robust companions." They are the strong bargemen.

"Thou are excellent at thy choice," Samias said. "But what pastime will thou use? None?"

A "pastime" is a hobby or source of entertainment.

"Yes, the quickest of all," Epiton said.

"What? Dice?" Samias asked.

"No," Epiton said. "When I am in haste, one-and-twenty games at chess, to pass a few minutes."

"A life for a little lord, and full of quickness," Dares said.

Epiton said:

"Tush, let me alone. Leave it to me.

"But I must necessarily see if I can find where Endymion lies, and then go to a certain fountain nearby, where they say faithful lovers shall have all things they will ask for.

"If I can find out any of these, *ego et magister meus erimus in tuto* — I and my master shall be friends. He is resolved to weep some three or four pailfuls to avoid the rheum of love that wambles — rolls around and rumbles — in his stomach."

Love is a rheum because it can produce watery discharges: tears. Many people hope that love is contagious.

Two watchmen and a constable entered the scene.

Cynthia had given these people the responsibility of guarding Endymion as he slept.

"Shall we never see thy master, Dares?" Samias asked.

"Yes, let us go now, for tomorrow Cynthia will be there," Dares said.

"I will go with you," Epiton said. "But how shall we get past the watchmen so we can see Endymion?"

Samias said:

"Tush, let me alone and leave it to me. I'll begin to speak to them."

He said to the two guardsmen and the constable:

"Masters, God speed you."

"God speed you" means "May God make you fortunate and successful."

"To speed" can also mean "to attain one's desire."

"Sir boy, we are all sped already," the first watchman said.

Epiton whispered to Samias and Dares, "So I think, for they all smell of drink like a beggar's beard."

They were drunk. That was their desire.

"But please, sirs, may we see Endymion?" Dares asked.

"No, we are commanded in Cynthia's name that no man shall see him," the second watchman said.

"No man?" Samias said. "Why, we are only boys."

The first watchman said to the other law enforcement officers, "By the Mass, neighbors, he says the truth. For if I swear I will never drink my liquor by the quart, and yet I call for two pints, I think with a safe conscience I may carouse and drink both."

Dares whispered to Samias and Epiton about the first watchman's speech: "Pithily, and to the purpose."

The second watchman said to the other law enforcement officers, "Tush, tush, neighbors, take me with you — let me understand you."

Samias whispered to Dares and Epiton, "This will grow hot. There will be an argument."

Dares whispered to Samias and Epiton, "Let them alone. Let them fight."

The second watchman said to the other law enforcement officers, "If I say to my wife, 'Wife, I will have no raisins in my pudding,' she puts in currants [small raisins]. Small raisins are raisins, and boys are men. Even as my wife should have put no raisins in my pudding, so there shall be no boys to see Endymion."

Dares whispered, "Learnedly."

He was sarcastic.

Epiton said, "Let Master Constable speak. I think he is the wisest among you."

In this society, constables had a reputation for having little wit and knowledge.

The constable said, "You know, neighbors, it is an old-said saw, an old and still-said proverb: 'Children and fools speak true.'"

"True," everyone said.

Hmm. Everyone who spoke "True" was saying that they were children and fools. The pages were children, and the guardsmen and the constable were fools.

"Well, there you see the men are the fools," the constable said, "because it is provided from the children."

Because they had spoken "True," the watchmen were either children or fools. Because the pages were boys, that left the designation of "fool" for the watchmen.

"Good," Dares said.

If the law enforcement officers were fools, they would let the pages see Endymion.

"Then I say, neighbors, that children must not see Endymion, because children and fools speak true," the constable said.

If the children were to succeed in giving the watchmen the designation of "fool," then the children would not be fools. Because the constable was a law-enforcement officer like the guardsmen, he did not want the pages to outwit the guardsmen, making them fools, and get to see Endymion.

"O, wicked application!" Epiton said.

It seemed that the law enforcement officers would not let the pages see Endymion.

"Scurvily brought about," Samias said.

The first watchman said to the pages:

"Nay, the constable says true; and therefore, until Cynthia shall have been here, Endymion shall not be uncovered."

Endymion was hidden away from the sight of other people by a curtain.

The first watchman then said to the pages:

"Therefore, go away."

Dares whispered to Samias and Epiton:

"A watch, said you? A man may watch seven years for a wise word and yet go without it. Their wits are all as rusty as their bills — their weapons."

Dares then said out loud:

"But come on, Master Constable, shall we have a song before we go?"

"With all my heart," the constable said.

The watchmen sang:

"*Stand, who goes there?*

"*We charge you [to] appear*

"'fore our constable here.

"In the name of the Man in the Moon,

"To us billmen [men armed with the long-handled bladed weapons called 'bills'] relate

"Why you stagger so late,

"And how you come [to be] drunk so soon."

The pages sang:

"What are ye, scabs?"

"Scabs" are "scoundrels."

The watchmen sang:

"This is the constable."

The pages sang:

"A patch [fool]."

The constable sang:

"Knock them down unless they all stand."

"Stand" means "Halt! Stand still!"

The constable continued to sing:

"If any run away,

"'tis the old watchman's play [trick]

"To reach him a bill of his hand."

The bill could be 1) a weapon, or 2) a handwritten legal document.

The pages sang:

"O gentlemen, hold [wait].

"Your gowns [a gown is a kind of outer garment] freeze with cold,

"And your rotten teeth dance [chatter] in your head."

Epiton sang:

"Wine nothing shall cost ye,"

Samias sang:

"Nor huge fires to roast ye."

The fires would also be free for the law enforcement officers.

Dares sang:

"Then soberly let us be led."

The pages were offering to buy the two guardsmen and the constable drinks. This was a way to get past the law enforcement officials, provided that the pages did not also become drunk.

The constable sang:

"*Come, my brown bills, we'll roar [carouse],*

"*Bounce [Knock] loud at tavern door,*"

"Brown bills" are the guardsmen, who carry the weapons called brown bills. Brown bills were either rusty or painted with brown paint. The guardmen's bills were rusty.

Everybody sang:

"*And i'th'morning steal all to bed.*"

They exited.

Endymion lay asleep on the lunary bank — the riverbank overgrown with lunary.

Alone, Corsites said to himself:

"I have come in sight of the lunary bank. Without doubt Tellus dotes upon me; and cunningly, so that I might not perceive her love, she has set me to do a task that is done before it is begun.

"Endymion, you must change your pillow, and if you are not weary of sleep, I will carry you where you shall sleep your fill at ease.

"It would be good that without more ceremonies I took him, lest being spied, I become entrapped and so incur the displeasure of Cynthia, who commonly sets a watch so that Endymion will have no wrong done to him."

The two watchmen and the constable were in an inn drinking with the pages.

Corsites tried to lift Endymion, but he could not.

Corsites said:

"What is this now, Endymion? Is your mastership — are you — so heavy? Or are you nailed to the ground? You don't stir one whit — one little bit!

"Then, Corsites, use all thy strength, although he will feel it and wake."

He again tried to lift Endymion, but he could not budge him.

Corsites said:

"What! Stone still? You have turned, I think, to earth, from lying so long on the earth.

"Didn't thou, Corsites, in front of Cynthia, pull up a tree that was fastened with roots and wreathed in knots to the ground for forty years? Didn't thou with main strength pull upon the iron gates that no battering ram or war machine could move?

"Have my weak thoughts made my strong arms brawn-fallen — shrunken and weak? Or is it the nature of love or the quintessence of the mind to breed numbness, or litherness — laziness — and languor, or I don't know what languishing in my joints and sinews, which are just the base strings of my body?

"Or does the remembrance of Tellus so refine my spirits into a matter so subtle and divine that the other fleshy parts cannot work while they — the refined spirits — muse?

"Rest thyself, rest thyself — nay, rend thyself in pieces, Corsites, and strive, in spite of love, fortune, and nature, to lift up this dulled body, heavier than dead and more senseless than death."

Some fairies entered the scene.

Corsites said to himself:

"But what are these so fair fiends that cause my hairs to stand upright and my spirits to fall down?"

He then said to the fairies:

"Hags —"

The fairies pinched him.

Corsites said:

"Ow! Alas!"

Corsites then tried to apologize:

"Nymphs, I beg your pardon."

The fairies again pinched him.

Corsites said:

"Aye me! Ow!"

"Aye me" is an expression of woe.

Corsites then asked himself:

"What am I doing here?"

The fairies danced, and as they sang a song, they pinched him, and Corsites fell asleep.

All the fairies sang:

"Pinch him, pinch him, black and blue.

"Saucy mortals must not view

"What the Queen of Stars is doing,

"Nor pry into our Fairy wooing."

The first fairy sang:

"Pinch him blue."

The second fairy sang:

"And pinch him black."

The third fairy sang:

"Let him not lack

"Sharp nails [fingernails] to pinch him blue and red,

"Till sleep has rocked his addle-head."

An addle-head is a muddled head.

The fourth fairy sang:

"For the trespass he has done,

"Spots o'er all his flesh shall run."

The fairies made spots on his face and hands.

The fourth fairy continued to sing:

"Kiss Endymion, kiss his eyes;

"Then [let's go] to our midnight hay-de-guise [midnight dance]."

They kissed Endymion and departed, leaving him and Corsites asleep.

Cynthia, Floscula, Semele, Panelion, Zontes, Pythagoras, and Gyptes talked together some distance away.

Floscula was Tellus' woman-servant.

Panelion and Zontes were lords at Cynthia's court.

Pythagoras was an ancient Greek philosopher, and Gyptes was an Egyptian soothsayer.

Cynthia said, "You see, Pythagoras, what ridiculous opinions you hold, and I don't doubt that you are now of another mind."

Pythagoras said, "Madam, I plainly perceive that the perfection of your brightness has pierced through the thickness that covered my mind, inasmuch that I am no less glad to be reformed than ashamed to remember my grossness."

"They are thrice fortunate who live in your palace, where truth is not in colors — false appearances — but in life, and virtues are not in imagination but in execution," Gyptes said.

Cynthia said:

"I have always endeavored to have living virtues rather than painted gods: to have the body of truth rather than have the tomb of truth.

"But let us walk to Endymion. Perhaps it lies in your arts to release him from the enchantment he is under.

"As for Eumenides, I fear that he is dead."

Eumenides had not yet returned from Thessaly.

"I have given all the natural reasons I can for such a long sleep," Pythagoras said.

"I can do nothing until I see him," Gyptes said.

"Come, Floscula, I am sure you are glad that you shall behold Endymion," Cynthia said.

"I would be blessed if I might have him recovered from his long sleep," Floscula said.

"Are you in love with his person?" Cynthia asked.

"No, but I am in love with his virtue," Floscula said.

"What do you say, Semele?" Cynthia asked.

"Madam, I dare say nothing for fear I offend," Semele said.

Cynthia said to Semele:

"It is likely that you cannot speak unless you are spiteful. But it is as good to be silent as it is to be saucy."

Cynthia then asked:

"Panelion, what punishment would be fit for Semele, in whose speech and thoughts are only contempt and sourness?"

Panelion replied, "I don't love, madam, to give any judgment. Yet since your Highness commands, I think that an appropriate punishment would be to commit her tongue close prisoner to her mouth."

Cynthia said:

"Agreed.

"Semele, if thou speak this twelve-month — this year — thou shall forfeit thy tongue.

She then said:

"Behold Endymion. Alas, poor gentleman, have thou spent thy youth in sleep, who once vowed all to my service? Hollow eyes? Grey hairs? Wrinkled cheeks? And decayed limbs? Is it destiny or deceit that has brought this to pass? If the first, who could prevent thy fate and its wretched stars? If the latter, I wish I might know thy cruel enemy.

"I favored thee, Endymion, for thy honor, thy virtues, thy affections. For the purpose only to bring thy thoughts within the compass of thy fortunes, I have seemed strange and unfriendly, I who might have stayed thee."

"Stayed" is ambiguous. It can mean 1) prevented, or 2) supported.

Cynthia continued:

"And now thy days are ended before my favor begins.

"But whom have we here? Isn't it Corsites?"

"It is, but more like a leopard than a man," Zontes said.

Cynthia ordered:

"Awaken him."

They awakened Corsites.

Cynthia said:

"How are things now, Corsites? What are you doing here?

"How did you come to be deformed?

"Look on thy hands, and then thou see the picture of thy face."

His hands and face were spotted like a leopard.

Corsites said:

"Miserable wretch, and accursed! How am I deluded?

"Madam, I ask pardon for my offense, and you see that my fortune deserves pity."

Cynthia said, "Speak on. Thy offense cannot deserve greater punishment than the spots you already have; but see that thou rehearse — speak — the truth, else thou shall not find me as thou wish me to be."

Corsites said:

"Madam, as it is no offense to be in love, being a mortal man, so I hope it can be no shame to tell with whom I am in love, my lady being heavenly.

"Your Majesty committed to my charge and responsibility the fair Tellus, whose beauty took my heart captive in the same moment that I undertook to carry her body prisoner.

"Since that time, I have found such combats in my thoughts between love and duty, reverence for you and affection for Tellus, that I could neither endure the conflict nor hope for the conquest."

Cynthia said, "In love? A thing far unfitting the name of a captain and, as I thought, the tough and unsmoothed nature of Corsites. But continue."

Corsites said:

"Feeling this continual war, I thought rather by parley — negotiation with an enemy — to yield than by certain danger to perish. I unfolded to Tellus the depth of my affections and directed my tongue to utter a sweet tale of love, my tongue that was accustomed to sound nothing but threats of war.

"She, too fair to be true and too false for one so fair, after a nice — coy — denial, practiced a notable deceit, commanding me to remove Endymion from this cabin and carry him to some dark cave, which seeking to accomplish, I found impossible, and so by fairies or fiends have been thus handled."

The "cabin" is the riverbank on which Endymion is lying. The trees offered some protection from the weather.

Cynthia said:

"What do you say, my lords? Isn't Tellus always practicing some deceits?

"Truly, Corsites, thy face is now too foul for a lover and thine heart is too fond — too foolish — for a soldier. You may see, when warriors become wantons, how their manners alter with their faces.

"Isn't it a shame, Corsites, that, having lived so long in Mars' camp, thou should now be rocked in Venus' cradle? Do thou wear Cupid's quiver at thy girdle, and make lances of looks?

"Well, Corsites, rouse thyself and be as thou have been, and let Tellus, who is made all of love, melt herself in her own looseness."

Corsites said, "Madam, I don't doubt but to recover my former state, for Tellus' beauty never wrought such love in my mind as now her deceit has wrought scorn in my mind; and yet to be revenged on a woman would be a thing more womanish than love itself."

"These spots, gentleman, are to be worn out if you rub them over with this lunary, so that in the place where you received this maim you shall find a medicine," Gyptes said.

"I thank you for that," Corsites said. "May the gods bless me and protect me from love and these pretty ladies — the fairies — who haunt this green!"

"Corsites, I wish that Tellus could see your amiable face," Floscula said.

"Amiable" means "worthy of being loved."

Corsites rubbed out his spots with lunary from the bank.

Forbidden to speak, Semele laughed.

"How spitefully Semele laughs, who dares not speak!" Zontes said.

"Couldn't you stir Endymion with that doubled strength of yours?" Cynthia asked Corsites.

A very strong man, Corsites had tried twice to move Endymion, the second time with all his strength.

"Not so much as his finger, even using all my strength," Corsites said.

Cynthia asked, "Pythagoras and Gyptes, what do you think about Endymion? What reason or cause is to be given for his sleep? What is the remedy?"

"Madam, it is impossible to give a reason for things that did not happen within the compass of nature," Pythagoras said. "It is very certain that some strange enchantment has bound all his senses."

"What do you say, Gyptes?" Cynthia asked.

Gyptes answered, "I agree with Pythagoras that it is enchantment, and an enchantment that is so strange that no art can undo it because heaviness argues a malice unremovable in the enchantress and heaviness argues that no power can end it until she who did it dies, or the heavens show some means of remedy more than miraculous."

"O Endymion, could spite itself devise a mischief so monstrous as to make thee dead with life, and living being altogether dead?" Floscula said. "Where others number their years, their hours, their minutes, and step to age by stairs, thou have thy years and times only in a cluster, being old before thou remembered thou were young."

Cynthia said:

"No more, Floscula; pity does him no good. I wish anything else might do him good, and I vow by the unspotted honor of a lady that he would not miss — lack —it.

"But is this, Gyptes, all that is to be done?"

"All that can be done as yet," Gyptes said. "It may be that either the enchantress shall die or else be identified. If either happens, I will then practice the utmost of my art. In the meantime, about this grove I would have a watch, and the first living thing that touches Endymion is to be arrested."

Cynthia asked, "Corsites, what do you say? Will you undertake to do this?"

"Good madam, pardon me," Corsites said. "I was overtaken — overcome — too recently. I would rather break into the midst of a main battle than fall again into the hands of those fair babies — those fairies."

Cynthia said:

"Well, I will provide others.

"Pythagoras and Gyptes, you shall yet remain in my court until I hear what may be done in this matter."

"We attend to and wait on you," Pythagoras said.

Cynthia said, "Let us go in."

They exited.

Endymion continued to sleep on the lunary bank, near a tree.

CHAPTER 5

— 5.1 —

Samias and Dares talked together.

Samias said, "Eumenides has told such strange tales that I may well wonder at them but never believe them."

Dares said:

"The other old man, what a sad speech he spoke, which caused us all almost to weep."

The two old men are the enchanted Endymion and the not enchanted Geron, who is "the other old man."

Dares continued:

"Cynthia is so desirous to know the experiment of her own virtue and to see if she has the power to awaken Endymion, and she is so willing to ease Endymion's hard fortune that she no sooner heard the discourse, but she got ready to try it and see the outcome."

Samias said:

"We will also see the outcome.

"But whist — hush! Here comes Cynthia with all her train of attendants. Let us sneak in among them."

Cynthia, Floscula, Semele, Panelion, Eumenides, Zontes, Gyptes, and Pythagoras entered the scene. Some attendants were also present.

Samias and Dares joined the throng.

Cynthia said, "Eumenides, it cannot sink into my head that I should be signified by that sacred fountain, for many things are there in the world to which those words may be applied."

"Good madam, agree just to try, else I shall think myself most unhappy that I did not ask for my sweet mistress," Eumenides said.

He had been allowed to have one wish granted by the fountain, and he had asked that Endymion be restored, not that Semele love him.

"Won't you tell me her name yet?" Cynthia asked.

"Pardon me, good madam, for if Endymion awakens, he shall tell her name to you. I myself have sworn never to reveal it," Eumenides said.

Cynthia said:

"Well, let us go to Endymion."

They approached the sleeping Endymion.

Cynthia continued:

"Good Endymion, I will not be so stately that I will not stoop to do thee good; and if thy liberty consists in a kiss from me, thou shall have it. And although my mouth has been heretofore as untouched as my thoughts, yet now to recover thy life (although to restore thy youth is impossible), I will do that to Endymion which yet never mortal man could boast of heretofore, nor shall ever hope for hereafter."

Cynthia kissed Endymion.

"Madam, he begins to stir," Eumenides said.

"Be quiet, Eumenides," Cynthia said. "Stand still."

"Ah, I see his eyes almost open," Eumenides said.

"I command thee once again, don't stir," Cynthia said. "I will stand before him."

"What do I see, Endymion almost awake?" Panelion asked.

Eumenides said, "Endymion, Endymion, are thou deaf or dumb? Or has this long sleep taken away thy memory? Ah, my sweet Endymion, don't thou see Eumenides, thy faithful friend, thy faithful Eumenides, who for thy safety has been taking care of his own contentment and happiness? Speak, Endymion, Endymion, Endymion!"

Groggy, Endymion said, "Endymion? I call to mind such a name. I remember that name."

Eumenides said:

"Have thou forgotten thyself, Endymion? Then I don't marvel that thou don't remember thy friend. Thou are Endymion, and I am Eumenides.

"Behold also Cynthia, by whose favor thou are awakened, and by whose virtue thou shall continue thy natural course of life."

"Endymion, speak, sweet Endymion," Cynthia said. "Don't thou know Cynthia?"

"O heavens, whom do I behold?" Endymion said. "Fair Cynthia, divine Cynthia?"

"I am Cynthia, and thou are Endymion," Cynthia said.

Looking at himself and feeling his face, Endymion said, "Endymion? What am I doing here? What! A long, gray beard? Hollow eyes? Withered body? Decayed limbs? And all in one night?"

Eumenides said, "One night? Thou have slept here for forty years, by what enchantress it is as yet not known. And look! The twig to which thou laid thy head has now become a tree. Can't thou remember Eumenides?"

Previously, Eumenides had spoken about Endymion sleeping for almost twenty years. Now he has spoken about him being asleep for forty years. Some time has passed, enough for people to travel to Thessaly, Greece, and Egypt and back. The twenty years and the forty years refer to how much Endymion has aged in his enchanted sleep. The others have aged only in accordance with non-magical, ordinary time. Of course, we learn that the twig Endymion slept by has become a mature tree, so it has also been affected by the enchantment.

Endymion said, "Thy name I do remember by the sound, but thy favor — thy features — I do not yet call to mind and remember. Only divine Cynthia, to whom time, fortune, destiny, and death are subject, I see and remember, and in all humility, I regard and reverence."

"You have good reason to remember Eumenides, who has for thy safety and sake forsaken his own solace," Cynthia said.

"Am I that Endymion who was accustomed in court to lead my life, and in jousts, tournaments, and weapons to exercise my youth?" Endymion asked. "Am I that Endymion?"

Eumenides said, "Thou are that Endymion, and I am Eumenides. Will thou not yet call me to remembrance?"

Endymion said, "Ah, sweet Eumenides, I now perceive thou are he, and that I myself have the name of Endymion. But I doubt that this should be my body; for how could my curled locks be turned to gray hairs and my strong body to a dying weakness, me having waxed and grown old and not knowing it?"

"Well, Endymion, arise," Cynthia said. "Sit down for a while, because thy limbs are stiff and not able to support thee, and tell us what thou have seen in thy sleep all this while. What dreams, visions, thoughts, and fortunes? For it is impossible but in so long a time thou should see strange things."

Endymion said, "Fair Cynthia, I will recite what I have seen, humbly desiring that when I exceed in length, you give me warning so that I may end my tale. For to utter all I have to speak would be troublesome, although perhaps the strangeness may somewhat abate the tediousness."

"Well, Endymion, begin," Cynthia said.

Endymion said:

"I thought that I saw a lady surpassingly beautiful but very evil, who in the one hand carried a knife with which she made a move as if to cut my throat, and in the other a looking glass, wherein seeing how ill anger became ladies, she refrained from intended violence. She was accompanied with other damsels, one of which, with a stern countenance, and as it were with a settled malice engraved in her eyes, provoked her to execute mischief. Another with a sad visage, and constant only in sorrow, with her arms crossed and watery eyes, seemed to lament my fortune, but dared not attempt to prevent the force."

In this society, crossed arms were a sign of melancholy.

Endymion continued:

"I started in my sleep, feeling my very veins to swell and my sinews to stretch with fear, and such a cold sweat bedewed all my body that death itself could not be as terrible as the vision."

"A strange sight," Cynthia said. "Gyptes at our better leisure shall expound it."

Endymion said: "After long debating with herself, mercy overcame anger, and there appeared in her heavenly face such a divine majesty, mingled with a sweet mildness, with the result that I was ravished with the sight above measure, and I wished that I might have enjoyed the sight without end. And so she departed with the other ladies, of whom the one retained still an unmovable cruelty, the other a constant pity."

Cynthia said, "Poor Endymion, how thou were frightened! What else?"

Endymion said:

"After her immediately appeared an aged man with a beard as white as snow, carrying in his hand a book with three leaves, and speaking, as I remember, these words: 'Endymion, receive this book with three leaves, in which are contained counsels, cunning policies and statecraft, and pictures.'

"And with that, he offered me the book, which I rejected; wherewith moved by a disdainful pity, he tore the first leaf into a thousand shivers — a thousand pieces. He offered it a second time, which I refused also; at which, bending his brows and fixing his eyes fast to the ground as though they were fixed to the earth and not again to be removed, then suddenly casting them up to the heavens, he tore in a rage the second leaf and offered me the book with only one leaf left.

"I don't know whether fear to offend or desire to know some strange thing moved me. I took the book, and so the old man vanished."

His memory was different from the dumb show the audience had witnessed. In the dumb show, there were three books. In his account, Endymion mentioned only one book with three leaves.

"What did thou imagine was in the last leaf?" Cynthia asked.

Endymion said:

"With a cold quaking in every joint, I beheld there — aye, portrayed to the life — many wolves barking at thee, Cynthia. The wolves, having ground their teeth to bite, did with striving bleed themselves to death.

"There I could see Ingratitude with a hundred eyes, looking for benefits for herself, and with a thousand teeth gnawing on the bowels wherein she was bred.

"Treachery stood all clothed in white, with a smiling countenance but with both her hands bathed in blood.

"Envy, with a pale and meager — emaciated — face, whose body was so lean that one might count all her bones, and whose garment was so tattered that it was easy to number every thread, stood shooting at stars, whose darts fell down again on her own face.

"There I could behold drones, or beetles, I don't know how to term them, creeping under the wings of a princely eagle, who, being carried into her nest, sought there to suck that vein that would have killed the eagle.

"I mused that things so base would attempt a deed so barbarous or would dare to imagine a thing so bloody.

"And I saw many other things, madam, the repetition whereof may at your better leisure seem more pleasing, for bees surfeit sometimes with honey, and the gods are glutted with harmony, and Your Highness may be dulled with delight."

The dream had been about political intrigue against Cynthia. It is difficult to see how hearing about more political intrigue could dull her with delight. Perhaps the rest of what Endymion had to say was about good things happening to Cynthia.

Cynthia said:

"I am content to be dieted; therefore, let us go in.

"Eumenides, see that Endymion will be well tended and taken care of, lest, either eating immoderately or sleeping again too long, he might fall into a deadly surfeit or into his former sleep.

"See that this also is proclaimed: that whosoever will expose this plot against Endymion shall have from Cynthia infinite thanks and no small rewards."

Cynthia exited, attended by her courtly entourage.

Floscula, Endymion, and Eumenides remained behind.

Floscula said, "Ah, Endymion, no one is as joyful as Floscula at thy restoring!"

Eumenides said:

"Yes, someone is more joyful than thee, Floscula. Let Eumenides be somewhat gladder, and don't do that wrong to the settled friendship of a man as to compare it with the light affection of a woman.

"Ah, my dear friend Endymion, allow me to die with gazing at thee!"

Endymion said, "Eumenides, thy friendship is immortal and not to be conceived and understood, and thy good will, Floscula, is better than I have deserved.

"But let us all wait on Cynthia. I marvel that Semele does not speak a word."

"Because if she does utter a word, she loses her tongue," Eumenides said.

"But how prospers your love?" Endymion asked.

"I have not yet spoken a word about it since your sleep," Eumenides said.

"I don't doubt that your affection is old and your appetite is cold," Endymion said.

Eumenides replied:

"No, Endymion, thine affection has made my affection stronger, and now my sparks have grown to flames and my amorous fancies have almost grown to frenzies.

"But let us follow Cynthia, and inside we will debate all this matter in detail."

They exited.

Sir Tophas and Epiton talked together.

"Epi, love has jostled my liberty from the wall and taken the upper hand of my reason," Sir Tophas said.

Elizabethan streets could be muddy, and whoever was closest to the street could be splashed with muddy water. Therefore, people wanted to stay close to the wall on the side of the street. When two men walking in opposite directions passed each other, the person with the higher social class was supposed to be closer to the wall.

Epiton said, "Let me then trip up the heels of your affection and thrust your good will into the gutter."

"No, Epi, love is a Lord of Misrule, and keeps Christmas in my corpse — in my body," Sir Tophas said.

The Lord of Misrule provided entertainment during the Christmas season at such places as the universities and the inns of court.

"No doubt there is good cheer and food," Epiton said. "What dishes of delight does his lordship feast you with?"

"His lordship" is a Lord of Misrule who is love.

Sir Tophas said, "First, with a great platter of plum-porridge of pleasure, wherein is stewed the mutton of mistrust."

"Excellent love-lap!" Epiton said. "Excellent love-pap!"

"Love-lap" is food that can be lapped up. "Pap" is soft baby food.

"Paps" are breasts, and "laps" are a locale of sexual goodies.

The word "plum" is bawdy. "Plum tree" was slang for a woman's crotch and thighs. "Climbing a plum tree" was slang for mounting and having sex with a woman.

"Stews" are brothels.

"Mutton" is slang for "prostitute."

Sir Tophas said, "Then comes a pie of patience, a hen of honey, a goose of gall, a capon of care, and many other viands, some sweet and some sour, which proves love to be as it was said of in old years: *dulce venenum* — a sweet poison."

A pie is a chattering, bold, impertinent person, male or female.

One thing that can be done with a pie is to have a finger in it.

A then-current meaning of "patience" is "permission" or "indulgence."

A "hen" is a woman or a wife, and both honey and female sexual arousal fluid are wet.

A "goose" is a fool.

"Gall" can mean asperity and rancor.

A capon is a castrated cock and is associated with a lack of manliness.

"Care" can mean worry.

The phrase "sweet poison" consists of two words that seem as if they ought not to belong together and yet can belong together.

Some of the words detailing the banquet can apply to Sir Tophas, and some of the words can apply to Dipsas.

"A brave banquet!" Epiton said.

Sir Tophas said, "But Epi, please feel my chin; something pricks me. What do thou feel or see?"

Examining his chin, Epiton said, "There are three or four little hairs."

"Please call it my beard," Sir Tophas said. "How I shall be troubled when this young spring shall grow to a great wood!"

A "spring" is a grove of trees.

Epiton said, "O, sir, your chin is but a quiller — a unfledged bird with a baby bird's fuzz — yet. You will be most majestic when it is fully fledged. But I marvel that you love Dipsas, that old crone."

Sir Tophas said, "*Agnosco veteris vestigia flamma.* I love the smoke of an old fire."

Agnosco veteris vestigia flamma means "I recognize the traces of the old flame."

Dido, Queen of Carthage, says this in Virgil's *Aeneid* when she recognizes that she is falling in love with the Trojan survivor Aeneas. The fire is old because she has felt it before: when she was married to her late husband.

"Why, she is so cold that no fire can thaw her thoughts," Epiton said.

Sir Tophas said:

"It is an old goose, Epi, that will eat no oats; old cows will kick, old rats gnaw cheese, and old sacks will have much patching.

"I prefer an old cony — an old rabbit — before a rabbit-sucker, aka suckling rabbit, and an ancient hen before a young chicken peeper."

Young chicks say, "Peep. Peep."

Epiton said:

"*Argumentum ab antiquitate*: an argument from antiquity."

Arguments from antiquity can be those based on myth or epic poems. People could apply lessons learned from Virgil's *Aeneid* or from Homer's *Iliad* and *Odyssey*.

Epiton then said to himself:

"My master loves antique work."

Sir Tophas loved both old works of literature and old women.

The argument from antiquity is this:

P1: A man quotes from old works of literature.

C: That man likes old women.

Sir Tophas said, "Give me a pippin that is withered like an old wife."

A pippin is a species of apple.

"Good, sir," Epiton said.

Sir Tophas said, "Then a *contrario sequitur argumentum*. Give me a wife who looks like an old pippin."

A contrario sequitur argumentum means "a contrary argument follows."

In other words:

P1: A pippin (a species of apple) resembles an old woman.

C: Therefore, an old woman resembles a pippin.

Epiton said to himself, "Nothing has made my master a fool except flat scholarship."

"Don't thou know that old wine is best?" Sir Tophas asked.

"Yes," Epiton said.

"And do thou know that like will to like?" Sir Tophas asked.

"Aye," Epiton said.

"And do thou know that Venus loved the best wine?" Sir Tophas asked.

"So," Epiton said.

Sir Tophas said, "Then I conclude that Venus was an old woman in an old cup of wine. For, *est Venus in vinis, ignis in igne fuit* — Venus is in wine as surely as fire is in fire."

This is his argument:

P1: Venus likes the best wine.

P2: The best wine is old.

P3: Like will to like.

C1: Venus is old.

P4: Venus is in wine as surely as fire is in fire.

C2: Venus is an old woman in a cup of old wine.

One problem with the argument is that the word "like" is used with different meanings. One is "enjoys"; the other is "similar."

"Like will to like" means "People are attracted to people who are similar to them."

Also, the word "in" is used with different senses: one metaphorical and the other literal.

Epiton said:

"*O lepidum caput*, O madcap master!"

O lepidum caput means, "Oh, witty mind."

"Madcap" is a play on the word *caput*, one meaning of which is "head."

Caps are worn on heads.

Epiton continued:

"You were worthy to win Dipsas, even if she were as old again as she is — that is, twice as old — for in your love you have worn the nap of your wit quite off and made it threadbare.

"But wait, who is coming here?"

Enter Samias and Dares.

Sir Tophas said, "My solicitors."

Sir Tophas had earlier asked the two pages to intercede for him with Dipsas.

Samias said, "All hail, Sir Tophas! how do you yourself feel?"

Sir Tophas answered, "Stately in every joint, which the common people term stiffness. Does Dipsas stoop? Will she yield? Will she bend?"

Dares said, "O, sir, as much as you would wish, for her chin almost touches her knees."

"Master, she is bent, I assure you," Epiton said.

Yes, she is bent almost double.

"What conditions does she ask?" Sir Tophas asked.

Samias said, "She has vowed she will never love any who does not have a tooth in his head fewer than she."

"How many teeth does she have?" Sir Tophas asked.

"One," Dares said.

"That goes hard, master, for then you must have no teeth," Epiton said.

Sir Tophas said, "It is a small request, and it agrees with the gravity of her years. What would a wise man do with his mouth full of bones like a charnel house — like a vault for bones? The true turtledove has no teeth."

Samias whispered to Epiton, "Thy master is in a notable mood, one in which he will lose his teeth to be like a turtledove."

Epiton whispered to Samias, "Let him lose his tongue, too. I don't care."

"Nay, you must also have no fingernails, for she long since has cast — shed — hers," Dares said.

Sir Tophas said, "That also I yield to. What a quiet life shall Dipsas and I lead, when we can neither bite nor scratch! You may see, youths, how age provides for peace."

Samias whispered to Epiton and Dares, "What shall we do to make him leave his love? For we never spoke to her."

Dares whispered to Samias:

"Let me alone. Leave it to me."

Dares then said out loud to Sir Tophas, "She is a notable witch, and she has turned her maid Bagoa into an aspen tree for revealing her secrets."

Sir Tophas said, "I honor her for her cunning, for now, when I am weary of walking on two legs, what a pleasure she may do me to turn me into some goodly ass and help me to have four legs!"

"Nay then," Dares said. "I must tell you the truth: Her husband, Geron, has come home, who for this past fifty years has had her as his wife."

Sir Tophas said:

"What do I hear? Has she a husband?

"Go to the sexton and tell him Desire is dead, and have him dig his — Desire's — grave.

"Oh heavens, a husband? What death is agreeable to — suits — my fortune?"

Samias said, "Don't be desperate, and we will help you to find a young lady."

Sir Tophas said:

"I love no Grissels — no young and immature girls; they are so brittle that they will crack like glass, or so dainty that if they are touched, they are immediately of the fashion of wax and bend out of shape.

"*Animus maioribus instat.* I desire old matrons."

Animus maioribus instat means "my spirit ventures greater themes."

Sir Tophas thought, however, that *maioribus* came from the noun *majores*, which means "ancestors." It actually comes from the adjective *maior*, which means "greater."

Sir Tophas continued:

"What a sight it would be to embrace one whose hair were as orient as the pearl, whose teeth shall be so pure a watchet — a pale blue — that they shall make the truest turquoise look stained, whose nose shall throw more beams from it than the fiery red carbuncle, whose eyes shall be environed about with redness exceeding the deepest coral, and whose lips might compare with silver for the paleness!"

A beautiful woman is unlikely to have pale blue teeth.

The lips — not the nose and eyes — of a beautiful woman are likely to be red.

Sir Tophas continued:

"If you can help me to such a one, I will by piecemeal curtail my affections towards Dipsas and walk my swelling thoughts until they are cold."

Epiton said to Sir Tophas:

"Wisely provided."

Epiton then said to the pages:

"What do you say, my friends? Will you angle — devise stratagems — for my master's cause?"

"Most willingly," Samias said.

Dares said, "If we don't quickly make him succeed, I will burn my cap. We will serve him with the spades, and we will dig an old wife out of the grave that shall be answerable to his gravity."

"Youths, adieu," Sir Tophas said. "He who brings me first news shall possess my inheritance."

He exited.

Dares said to Epiton, "What! Does thy master own land?"

"Don't you know that my master is *liber tenens*?" Epiton asked.

The Latin is bad.

"What's that?" Samias asked.

"A freeholder," Epiton said. "But I will go after him."

Samias said, "And we will go to hear the news about Endymion. Things are coming to a conclusion."

All exited.

Panelion and Zontes talked together.

Panelion said, "Who would have thought that Tellus, being so fair by nature, so honorable by birth, so wise by education, would have entered into an evil to the gods so odious, to men so detestable, and to her friend so malicious?"

The word "friend" means "man who loves her."

Zontes said, "If Bagoa had not revealed it, how then would it have come to light? But we see that gold and fair words have the strength to corrupt the strongest men, and therefore they are able to work silly, foolish women like wax."

I wonder what Cynthia will decide in this case," Panelion said.

Zontes said, "I fear that she will do what she does in all cases: Hear of it in justice and then judge of it in mercy. For how can it be that she who is unwilling to punish her deadliest foes with disgrace will revenge the injuries and crimes of her train of attendants with death?"

Panelion said:

"That old witch Dipsas, in a rage, having understood her crafty practice to be revealed, turned poor Bagoa into an aspen tree.

"But let us make haste and bring Tellus before Cynthia, for she was coming out after us."

"Let us go," Zontes said.

They exited.

Cynthia, Semele, Floscula, Dipsas, Endymion, Eumenides, Geron, Pythagoras, Gyptes, and Sir Tophas met together at the lunary riverbank where a tree stood.

Cynthia said, "Dipsas, thy years of age are not as many as thy vices, yet they are more in number than commonly nature affords, or justice should permit. Have thou almost these fifty years practiced that detested wickedness of witchcraft? Were thou so simple as not to know the nature of simples, thou who of all creatures are the most sinful?"

These simples are herbs used in magic.

Cynthia continued:

"Thou have threatened to turn my course awry and alter by thy damnable art the government that I now possess by the eternal gods. But know thou, Dipsas, and let all the enchanters know, that Cynthia, being placed for light on earth, is also protected by the powers of heaven.

"Thou may breathe out words and curses and spells, thou may gather herbs, thou may find out stones and minerals agreeable to thine art, yet thou will have no force to appall my heart, in which courage is so rooted, and constant persuasion of the mercy of the gods is so grounded that I esteem all thy witchcraft as weak as the world esteems thy case wretched.

"This noble gentleman, Geron, who was once thy husband but is now thy mortal — deadly — hate, thou did contrive to make him live in a deserted, uninhabited area, almost desperate.

"Thou have bewitched by art Endymion, the flower of my court and the hope of succeeding time, before thou would allow him to flourish by nature."

Dipsas replied:

"Madam, things past may be repented, not recalled. There is nothing so wicked that I have not done, nor is there anything so wished-for as death. Yet among all the things that I have committed, there is nothing that as much torments my rent — my torn — and ransacked thoughts as that in the prime of my husband's youth, I divorced him by my devilish art, for which, if to die might be amends, I would not live until tomorrow. If for me to live and be still more miserable would better content him, I would wish of all creatures to be the oldest and ugliest."

Mythology has tales of mortals asking to live many, many years more than is normal, but forgetting to ask for endless youth. Such mortals grow older and older, and when one such mortal, a Sibyl, was asked what she wished for most, she wished for death. Dipsas is wise enough to know that asking for an excessively long life is a punishment.

Geron said, "Dipsas, thou have made this difference between Endymion and me: Both he and I being young, thou have caused me to remain awake in melancholy, losing the joys of my youth, and thou have caused him to sleep, not remembering youth."

"Wait, here comes Tellus," Cynthia said. "We shall now know all."

Corsites and Tellus entered the scene along with Panelion and Zontes.

Corsites said to Tellus, "I wish that to Cynthia thou could make as good an excuse in truth as to me thou have done by wit."

"Truth shall be my answer, and therefore I will not search for an excuse," Tellus replied.

Cynthia said:

"Is it possible, Tellus, that so few years — so short a time, and so young a person — should harbor so many evil deeds?

"I have borne thy swelling pride because it is a thing that beauty excuses and makes blameless — beauty that the more it exceeds fairness in measure and goes beyond normal beauty, the more it stretches itself and swells itself in disdain."

A proverb stated, "Where beauty is, there needs [be] no other plea."

Cynthia continued:

"I smile at thy devices and plots against Corsites because the sharper wits are, the shrewder they are.

"But this unacquainted — strange and unheard of — and most unnatural practice and conspiracy with a vile enchantress against so noble a gentleman as Endymion I abhor as a thing most malicious, and I will revenge it as a deed most monstrous.

"And as for you, Dipsas, I will send you into the desert among wild beasts, and I will see whether you can cast lions, tigers, boars, and bears into as dead a sleep as you did Endymion, or turn them into trees as you have done Bagoa."

Dipsas will have to defend her life against wild beasts.

Cynthia continued:

"But tell me, Tellus, what was the cause of this cruel conduct, far unbefitting thy sex, in which there should be nothing but simpleness and innocence, and which is much disagreeing from thy face, in which nothing seemed to be but softness?"

Tellus said, "Divine Cynthia, by whom I receive my life and by whom I am content to end it, I can neither excuse my fault without lying nor confess it without shame. Yet if it were possible that in as heavenly thoughts as yours there could fall such earthly emotions and thoughts as mine, I would then hope, if not to be pardoned without extreme punishment, yet to be heard without great marvel."

"Speak on, Tellus," Cynthia said. "I cannot imagine anything that can color — render acceptable — such a cruelty as you have shown."

Tellus said:

"Endymion, that Endymion, in the prime of his youth, so ravished my heart with love that I could not find means to obtain my desires, nor could I find reason to resist them.

"What woman did not love Endymion, who was young, wise, honorable, and virtuous? Besides, what metal and mettle — material and temperament — was that woman made of, being mortal, who is not affected with the spice, and not infected with the poison of that not-to-be-expressed yet always-to-be-felt love, which breaks the brains and never bruises and hurts the brow and forehead, consumes the heart and never touches the skin, and makes a deep scar to be felt before any wound at all can be seen?

"My heart, too tender to withstand such a divine fury, yielded to love. Madam, not without blushing, I confess that I yielded to love."

Cynthia said:

"A strange effect of love, to work such an extreme hate.

"What do you say, Endymion? Was all this for love?"

Endymion said, "I say, madam, if this was a woman's love, then I pray that the gods send me a woman's hate."

If love caused Tellus to treat him like this, then he would prefer that Tellus hate him.

Cynthia said:

"That would be as bad, for then by a contrary argument, you would never sleep."

If a woman's love had made him sleep continually, then a woman's hate would make him stay awake continually.

Cynthia then said:

"But continue, Tellus. Let us hear the end."

Tellus said:

"Feeling a continual burning in all my bowels and a bursting in almost every vein, I could not smother the inward fire, but it must necessarily be perceived by the outward smoke; and by the flying abroad of many sparks, many people judged that I had scalding flames.

"Endymion, as full of art as wit, marking my eyes (in which he might see almost his own), my sighs (by which he might always hear his name sounded), aimed at my heart (in which he was assured his person was imprinted), and by questions wrung out that which was ready to burst out.

"When he saw the depth of my affections, he swore that my affections in comparison to his were as fumes to Etna, valleys to Alps, ants to eagles, and nothing could be compared to my beauty but his love and eternity.

"Thus, drawing a smooth shoe upon a crooked foot, he made me believe that (which all of our sex willingly acknowledge and believe) I was beautiful, and to wonder (which indeed is a thing miraculous) that any of his sex should be faithful."

"Endymion, how will you clear yourself?" Cynthia asked.

"Madam, by my own accuser," Endymion answered.

Cynthia said, "Well, Tellus, proceed, but briefly, lest, taking delight in uttering thy love, thou offend us with the length of it."

Tellus said:

"I will, madam, quickly make an end of my love and my tale.

"Finding continual increase of my tormenting thoughts, and finding that the enjoying and experiencing of my love made deeper wounds than the entering into it, I could find no means to ease my grief but to follow Endymion, and continually to have him before my eyes, who had me as a slave and subject to his love.

"But in the moment that I feared his falsehood, and fried myself most in my affections, I found (ah, grief, even then I lost myself) him cursing his stars, his state, the earth, the heavens, the world in the most melancholy and desperate terms, and all for love of —"

She hesitated.

"Of whom?" Cynthia said. "Tellus, speak boldly."

"Madam, I dare not utter the name for fear of offending," Tellus said.

"Speak, I say," Cynthia said. "Who will dare to take offense if thou are commanded by Cynthia to speak?"

Tellus said, "For the love of Cynthia."

Cynthia said:

"For my love, Tellus? That would be strange.

"Endymion, is it true?"

"It is true in all things, madam," Endymion said. "Tellus does not speak falsely."

Cynthia said, "What will this breed to and develop into in the end? Well, Endymion, we shall hear all."

Tellus said:

"Seeing my hopes turned to mishaps and a settled dissembling towards me by Endymion, and his unmovable desire for Cynthia, and forgetting both myself and my sex, I fell into this unnatural hate.

"For knowing your virtues, Cynthia, to be immortal, I couldn't imagine that I would be able to draw him to me, and finding my own affections unquenchable, I could not bear the thought that anyone else should possess what I had pursued.

"For although in majesty, beauty, virtue, and dignity, I always humbled and yielded myself to Cynthia, yet in affections I esteemed myself equal with the goddesses, and I esteemed all other creatures, according to their states, with myself. For stars in proportion to their bigness have their lights, and the sun has no more. And little pitchers, when they can hold no more, are as full as great vessels that run over.

"Thus, madam, in all truth I have uttered the unhappiness of my love and the cause of my hate, yielding wholly to that divine judgment which never erred for lack of wisdom or envied for too much partiality."

Cynthia asked:

"What do you say, my lords, about this matter?

"But what do you say, Endymion? Has Tellus told the truth?"

Endymion answered, "Madam, in all things except in that she said I loved her and swore to honor her."

Certainly, he had misled Tellus and made her believe that he loved and honored her.

Cynthia asked, "Was there such a time when for my love thou did vow thyself to death, and in respect of it loathed thy life? Speak, Endymion. I will not revenge it with hate."

Endymion said:

"The time was, madam, and is, and ever shall be, that I honored Your Highness above all the world; but I never dared to stretch it so far as to call it love.

"No one has pleased my eye but Cynthia.

"No one has delighted my ears but Cynthia.

"No one has possessed my heart but Cynthia.

"I have forsaken all other fortunes to follow Cynthia.

"And here I stand ready to die if it pleases Cynthia.

"Such a difference has the gods set between our states that all must be duty, loyalty, and reverence; nothing, unless Your Highness permits it, shall be termed love.

"Let my unspotted thoughts, my languishing body, and my discontented life obtain by princely favor that which to demand as a right they must not presume, only wishing for impossibilities.

"With the imagination of having these impossibilities, I will spend my spirits, and I will softly call it love to myself, so that no creature may hear. And if anyone urges me to utter what I whisper, then I will name it honor: My love is honorable.

"If I am not driven from this sweet contemplation, I shall live of all men the most content, taking more pleasure in my aged thoughts than I ever did in my youthful actions."

Cynthia said:

"Endymion, this honorable respect of thine shall be christened love in thee, and my reward to give you for it shall be my favor. Persevere, Endymion, in loving me; I account more strength in a true heart than in a walled city.

"I have labored to win all, and I work to keep such as I have won; but those whom neither my favor can move to continue constant and loyal, nor my offered benefits can get to be faithful, the gods shall either bring to truth or shall revenge their treacheries with justice.

"Endymion, continue as thou have begun, and thou shall find that Cynthia does not shine on thee in vain."

Endymion's youthful looks were restored to him, although earlier (5.1) Cynthia had said that restoring his youth was impossible. Cynthia's powers, she is discovering, are stronger than she had believed them to be.

Endymion said, "Your Highness has blessed me, and your words have again restored my youth. I think I feel my joints strong, and these moldy hairs to molt, and all by your virtue, Cynthia, into whose hands are committed the balance that weighs time and fortune."

[When the actor said, "these moldy hairs to molt," he took off a wig and a fake beard.]

Cynthia said:

"What! Young again?

"Then it is a pity to punish Tellus."

Tellus said, "Ah, Endymion, now that I know thee, I ask pardon from thee. Allow me always to wish thee well."

"Tellus, Cynthia must command what she will," Endymion said.

"Endymion, I rejoice to see thee in thy former state," Floscula said.

"Good Floscula, to thee also I am in my former affections," Endymion said.

Eumenides said, "Endymion, the comfort of my life, how I am ravished with a matchless joy, saving only the enjoying of my mistress!"

Cynthia said, "Endymion, you must now tell whom Eumenides shrines for his saint."

Eumenides had previously stated that he could not name whom he loved, but that Endymion could reveal the secret.

Endymion answered, "Semele, madam."

Cynthia asked, "Semele, Eumenides? Is it Semele? The very wasp of all women, whose tongue stings as much as an adder's tooth?"

"It is Semele, Cynthia," Eumenides said. "Only the possessing of her love can prolong my life. I can't live without her."

Cynthia said:

"Since Endymion is restored, we will have all parties pleased.

"Semele, are you happy after so long trial of his faith, such rare secrecy, such unspotted love, to take Eumenides?

"Why don't you speak? Not a word?"

"Silence, madam, consents," Endymion said. "That is most true."

"It is true, Endymion," Cynthia said. "Eumenides, take Semele. Take her, I say."

"I give you my humble thanks, madam," Eumenides said. "Only now do I begin to live."

Semele said to Cynthia:

"A hard choice, madam: either to be married if I say nothing, or to lose my tongue if I speak a word. Yet I choose to have my tongue cut out rather than to have my heart distempered and vexed.

"I will not have him."

Cynthia said:

"So speaks the parrot?"

She was calling Semele a parrot-like chatterer.

Cynthia continued:

"She shall nod hereafter with signs. Cut off her tongue; nay, cut off her head, the head of her who, having a servant — a wooer — of honorable birth, honest manners, and true love, will not be persuaded to have him!"

Semele said, "He is no faithful lover, madam, for if he were, then he would have asked for his mistress when he peered into the fountain."

His mistress was the woman he loved: Semele.

Geron said, "Had he not been faithful, he would have never seen into the fountain, and so he would have lost his friend Endymion *and* he would have lost his mistress, Semele."

Eumenides said:

"Thine own thoughts, sweet Semele, witness against thy words, for what have thou found in my life but love? And as yet what have I found in my love but bitterness?"

He then said to Cynthia:

"Madam, pardon Semele, and let my tongue ransom hers."

Cynthia said:

"Thy tongue, Eumenides? Why would thou live, lacking a tongue to blaze and proclaim the beauty of Semele?

"Well, Semele, I will not command love, for it cannot be compelled. Let me entreat it."

Semele said:

"I am content that Your Highness shall command, for only just now do I think Eumenides faithful, who is willing to lose his tongue for my sake, yet he is loath to lose it because it would do me better service by proclaiming my beauty.

"Madam, I accept Eumenides as my husband."

"I thank you, Semele," Cynthia said.

Eumenides said:

"Ah, happy Eumenides, who has a friend so faithful and a mistress so fair! With what sudden trouble will the gods daunt and subdue this excess of joy?"

This society believed that the pagan gods punished people who experienced an excess of joy.

Eumenides then said:

"Sweet Semele, I live or die as thou will order me."

Cynthia said:

"What shall become of Tellus?

"Tellus, you know that Endymion is vowed to a service from which death cannot remove him.

"Corsites still casts a loving look towards you. What do you say? Will you have your Corsites and so receive pardon for all that is past?"

"Madam, most willingly," Tellus said.

"But I cannot tell whether Corsites is agreeable to this," Cynthia said.

"Aye, I am, madam," Corsites said. "I am happier to enjoy Tellus than I would be to enjoy the monarchy of the world."

Eumenides said, "Why, she caused you to be pinched by fairies."

"Aye, but her fairness — her beauty — has pinched my heart more deeply," Corsites said.

Cynthia said:

"Well, enjoy thy love.

"But what have you wrought in the castle, Tellus?"

Tellus had been ordered to embroider while she was a prisoner in the castle.

Tellus answered, "Only the picture of Endymion."

"Then possess and play with as much of Endymion as his picture comes to," Cynthia said.

Corsites said, "Ah, my sweet Tellus, my love shall be as thy beauty is: matchless."

Cynthia said, "Now this remains, Dipsas: If thou will forswear that vile art of enchanting, Geron has promised again to receive thee; otherwise, if thou are wedded to that wickedness, I must and will see it punished to the utmost."

Dipsas said, "Madam, I renounce both the substance and the shadow of that most horrible and hateful trade, vowing continual penance to the gods, and obedience to Your Highness."

"What do you say, Geron?" Cynthia asked. "Will you allow her to be your wife?"

Geron said:

"Aye, with more joy than I did marry her the first day; for nothing could happen to make me happy except only her forsaking that mean, base, and detestable course.

"Dipsas, I embrace thee."

Dipsas said, "And I embrace thee, Geron, to whom I will hereafter recite the cause of these my first follies."

They embraced.

Cynthia said, "Well, Endymion, nothing remains now except that we depart. Thou have my favor, Tellus has her friend and lover, Eumenides is in paradise with his Semele, and Geron is contented with Dipsas."

Sir Tophas said, "Nay, wait. I cannot handsomely go to bed without Bagoa."

Cynthia said, "Well, Sir Tophas, it may be that there are more virtues in me than I myself know of, for I awakened Endymion, and at my words he grew young. I will see whether I can turn this tree again into thy true love."

Sir Tophas said, "Turn her into a true love or a false love. I don't care as long as she is a wench."

Cynthia said, "Bagoa, Cynthia puts an end to thy hard fortunes, for being turned into a tree for revealing a truth. I will recover thee again if the effect of truth is in my power."

Bagoa had revealed Dipsas' secrets and Dipsas responded by turning her into a tree. If Bagoa were under Cynthia's protection, Dipsas would not have been able to turn Bagoa into a tree, so perhaps Bagoa did not reveal Dipsas' secrets to Cynthia but to others.

The aspen tree transformed back into Bagoa.

Looking at her, Sir Tophas said. "This is Bagoa? A bots — a plague — upon thee!"

He did not like what he saw.

Is it possible that Bagoa was young and beautiful?

Sir Tophas preferred old women.

Cynthia said:

"Come, my lords, let us go in.

"You, Gyptes and Pythagoras, if you yourselves cannot be happy in our court to fall away from the vain follies of philosophers and practice such virtues as are here practiced, you shall be entertained according to your deserts, for Cynthia is no stepmother to strangers."

If they practice virtue, they will be treated well because she is not like an evil stepmother. If they don't, they will be treated as they ought to be treated.

"I had rather spend ten years in Cynthia's court than one hour in Greece," Pythagoras said.

"And I choose rather to live by the sight of Cynthia than by the possessing of all Egypt," Gyptes said.

"Then follow me," Cynthia said.

Eumenides said, "We all attend on you."

All exited.

EPILOGUE

The Epilogue said:

"A man walking abroad, the wind and sun strove for sovereignty: the one with his blast, the other with his beams. The wind blew hard; the man wrapped his garment about him harder. It blustered more strongly; he then girt it fast — wrapped it tight — to him. 'I cannot prevail,' said the wind. The sun, casting her crystal beams, began to warm the man; he unloosed his gown. Yet it shined brighter; he then put it off. 'I yield,' said the wind, 'for if thou continue shining, he will also put off his coat.'

"Dread sovereign, the malicious who seek to overthrow us with threats only stiffen our thoughts and make them sturdier in storms. But if Your Highness vouchsafe with your favorable beams to glance upon us, we shall not only stoop, but with all humility lay both our hands and hearts at Your Majesty's feet."

— NOTES —

A Dumb Show

- The three ladies are possibly Tellus, who wants to hurt Endymion; Dipsas, who enchants Endymion; and Bagoa, who would like to protect Endymion. Other interpretations, including allegorical interpretations, are possible.

- Geron, who has not appeared in this book at the time of the dumb show, is the old man.

- The Cumaean Sibyl wrote prophecies on leaves, and she placed them at the mouth of the cave she lived in — a cave that was one of the entrances to the Land of the Dead. Sometimes, the wind scattered the leaves, and she made no attempt to put them back in the correct order. But sometimes, they were collected into books.

The Sibyl went to King Tarquin II of Rome and offered to sell to him nine books of prophecies at a high price. He refused to buy them, and the Sibyl burned three of the books and offered the remaining six books at the same high price. Again, he refused to buy them, and the Sibyl burned three of the books and offered the remaining three books at the same high price. This time, King Tarquin II bought the books.

— 3.4 —

GERON:
> *You doted, then, not loved. For affection is grounded*
> *on virtue and virtue is never peevish; or on beauty, and*
> *beauty loveth to be praised.*
> (3.4.64-66)

Source of Above: Lyly, John. *Endymion*. Edited by David Bevington. New York: Manchester University Press, 1996. P. 133.

"Affection" means love. It may seem superficial for love to be grounded on beauty, but it need not be. Often, a husband's conception of beauty changes as his wife's body changes, whether through pregnancy or age or some other cause.

A few examples:

"*Men Of Reddit, Is It Boring To See Your Girlfriend / Wife's Naked Body After A While Of Being Together? Why Or Why Not?*"

1) Child_of_Lake_Bodom wrote, "Almost ten years now, still not tired of it."

2) kaljupaa wrote, "Married almost 18 years and still can't get enough of her."

3) CaptainFrivolous wrote, "No, I just wish she believed me and would show it a little more."

4) mister-fancypants- wrote, "My girlfriend will flash me basically anytime I say, 'Lemme see them titties.'"

5) Lumberjack1286 wrote:

"No, because boobs.

"Edit: Of course, a comment about boobs is going to be my most-upvoted comment."

6) KrustyKrabPizzaLover wrote, "Nah. She's still as beautiful as she was 20 years ago."

7) PerfectionPending wrote, "Not at all. Been married 18 years, and I can't help but stare when she changes. I just stop whatever I'm doing and blatantly stare. She smiles a shy flattered smile and continues changing. I'll often tell her somewhere in there how beautiful she is."

8) Whole-Box537 wrote, "You can chill and be naked together in a non-sexual way, and when things heat up, it's as good as it ever was."

9) thingsmykidsdraw asked, "Why are all these comments so wholesome?"

coolbeansbradley commented, "It's a nice start to my day. Giving me hope."

213x4s commented, "I was not expecting this wholesome level at all."

10) JohnyAngelo wrote, "I think boring is too strong of a word. You get accustomed to seeing it … think about good food, you know how it tastes and looks so it's not surprising to you anymore but you still wanna eat it every chance you get."

11) bobbyray89 wrote:

"Been with my wife for 13 years. I still get giddy when it's sexy time.

"I will say, I was surprised that my taste changed from when we were young to now after kids. She's built like a mother of three and I dig it."

fooliemon commented, "When the body changes are because she made your kids, it's like the changes are badges of honor in your life together."

12) diskootdatkoot wrote, "The more deeply I grow a relationship with my partner the more I see their body as a beautiful work of art that I know intimately."

13) readit2U wrote, "Been with my wife for 36 years and she still turns me on. She doesn't understand why, but she is glad."

Dnasty12-12 commented, "Agree ... 39 years together here ... new grandparents ... I tell her the best part of being grandparents is watching her bend over as she picks up toys all over the floor."

14) ulittlerippa wrote, "Partner is so pregnant she's ready to pop ... cellulite, weight gain ... and it's the most beautiful I've ever seen her. And yes, I tell her that. She's growing our child, and it's magnificent."

Source: throwawayacc9q7, "Men of Reddit, is it boring to see your girlfriend/wife's naked body after a while of being together? Why or why not?" Reddit. AskReddit. 10 January 2021 < https://www.reddit.com/r/AskReddit/comments/s0catu/men_of_reddit_is_it_boring_to_see_your/ >.

EPILOGUE

For Your Information:

THE SUN AND THE WIND
Phebus and Boreas from on high
Upon the road a Horseman spy,
Wearing a cloak for fear of rain.
Says Boreas, "His precaution's vain
'Gainst me, I'll shew you for a joke
How soon I'll make him quit his cloak."
"Come on," says Phebus, "let us see
Who best succeeds, or [either] you or me."
The Wind to blow so fierce began,
He almost had unhors'd his man;
But still the cloak, for all his roar,
Was wrapp'd more closely than before.
When Boreas what he could had done,
"Now for my trial," says the Sun,
And with his beams so warm'd the air.
The Man his mantle could not bear.
But open'd first, then threw aside.
[Moral:]
Learn hence, unbending sons of pride,
Persuasive manners will prevail.
When menaces and bluster fail.

Source: Sir B. Boothby, *Fables and Satires*. Fable III.
Imitated from Avicenus.
https://archive.org/stream/fablesandsatire01bootgoog/
fablesandsatire01bootgoog_djvu.txt
For Your Information:

The Wind and the Sun were disputing which was the stronger.
Suddenly they saw a traveller coming down the road, and the Sun

said: *"I see a way to decide our dispute. Whichever of us can cause that traveller to take off his cloak shall be regarded as the stronger. You begin." So the Sun retired behind a cloud, and the Wind began to blow as hard as it could upon the traveller. But the harder he blew the more closely did the traveller wrap his cloak round him, till at last the Wind had to give up in despair. Then the Sun came out and shone in all his glory upon the traveller, who soon found it too hot to walk with his cloak on.*

[Moral:]

Kindness effects more than severity.

Source: Aesop. "The Wind and the Sun." https://etc.usf.edu/lit2go/pdf/passage/697/aesops-fables-085-the-wind-and-the-sun.pdf

APPENDIX A: FAIR USE

§ 107. Limitations on exclusive rights: Fair use
   Release date: 2004-04-30

Notwithstanding the provisions of sections 106 and 106A, the fair use of a copyrighted work, including such use by reproduction in copies or phonorecords or by any other means specified by that section, for purposes such as criticism, comment, news reporting, teaching (including multiple copies for classroom use), scholarship, or research, is not an infringement of copyright. In determining whether the use made of a work in any particular case is a fair use the factors to be considered shall include —

(1) the purpose and character of the use, including whether such use is of a commercial nature or is for nonprofit educational purposes;

(2) the nature of the copyrighted work;

(3) the amount and substantiality of the portion used in relation to the copyrighted work as a whole; and

(4) the effect of the use upon the potential market for or value of the copyrighted work.

The fact that a work is unpublished shall not itself bar a finding of fair use if such finding is made upon consideration of all the above factors.

Source of Fair Use information:

http://www.law.cornell.edu/uscode/17/107.html

APPENDIX B: ABOUT THE AUTHOR

It was a dark and stormy night. Suddenly a cry rang out, and on a hot summer night in 1954, Josephine, wife of Carl Bruce, gave birth to a boy — me. Unfortunately, this young married couple allowed Reuben Saturday, Josephine's brother, to name their first-born. Reuben, aka "The Joker," decided that Bruce was a nice name, so he decided to name me Bruce Bruce. I have gone by my middle name — David — ever since.

Being named Bruce David Bruce hasn't been all bad. Bank tellers remember me very quickly, so I don't often have to show an ID. It can be fun in charades, also. When I was a counselor as a teenager at Camp Echoing Hills in Warsaw, Ohio, a fellow counselor gave the signs for "sounds like" and "two words," then she pointed to a bruise on her leg twice. Bruise Bruise? Oh yeah, Bruce Bruce is the answer!

Uncle Reuben, by the way, gave me a haircut when I was in kindergarten. He cut my hair short and shaved a small bald spot on the back of my head. My mother wouldn't let me go to school until the bald spot grew out again.

Of all my brothers and sisters (six in all), I am the only transplant to Athens, Ohio. I was born in Newark, Ohio, and have lived all around Southeastern Ohio. However, I moved to Athens to go to Ohio University and have never left.

At Ohio U, I never could make up my mind whether to major in English or Philosophy, so I got a bachelor's degree with a double major in both areas, then I added a Master of Arts degree in English and a Master of Arts degree in Philosophy. Yes, I have my MAMA degree.

Currently, and for a long time to come (I eat fruits and veggies), I am spending my retirement writing books such as *Nadia Comaneci: Perfect 10*, *The Funniest People in Comedy*, *Homer's* Iliad: *A Retelling in Prose*, and *William Shakespeare's* Hamlet: *A Retelling in Prose*.

If all goes well, I will publish one or two books a year for the rest of my life. (On the other hand, a good way to make God laugh is to tell Her your plans.)

By the way, my sister Brenda Kennedy writes romances such as *A New Beginning* and *Shattered Dreams*.

APPENDIX C: SOME BOOKS BY DAVID BRUCE

Retellings of a Classic Work of Literature

Arden of Faversham: *A Retelling*

Ben Jonson's The Alchemist: *A Retelling*

Ben Jonson's The Arraignment, or Poetaster: *A Retelling*

Ben Jonson's Bartholomew Fair: *A Retelling*

Ben Jonson's The Case is Altered: *A Retelling*

Ben Jonson's Catiline's Conspiracy: *A Retelling*

Ben Jonson's The Devil is an Ass: *A Retelling*

Ben Jonson's Epicene: *A Retelling*

Ben Jonson's Every Man in His Humor: *A Retelling*

Ben Jonson's Every Man Out of His Humor: *A Retelling*

Ben Jonson's The Fountain of Self-Love, or Cynthia's Revels: *A Retelling*

Ben Jonson's The Magnetic Lady, or Humors Reconciled: *A Retelling*

Ben Jonson's The New Inn, or The Light Heart: *A Retelling*

Ben Jonson's Sejanus' Fall: *A Retelling*

Ben Jonson's The Staple of News: *A Retelling*

Ben Jonson's A Tale of a Tub: *A Retelling*

Ben Jonson's Volpone, or the Fox: *A Retelling*

Christopher Marlowe's Complete Plays: Retellings

Christopher Marlowe's Dido, Queen of Carthage: *A Retelling*

Christopher Marlowe's Doctor Faustus: *Retellings of the 1604 A-Text and of the 1616 B-Text*

Christopher Marlowe's Edward II: *A Retelling*

Christopher Marlowe's The Massacre at Paris: *A Retelling*

Christopher Marlowe's The Rich Jew of Malta: *A Retelling*

Christopher Marlowe's Tamburlaine, Parts 1 and 2: *Retellings*

Dante's Divine Comedy: *A Retelling in Prose*

Dante's Inferno: *A Retelling in Prose*

Dante's Purgatory: *A Retelling in Prose*

Dante's Paradise: *A Retelling in Prose*

The Famous Victories of Henry V: *A Retelling*

From the Iliad *to the* Odyssey: *A Retelling in Prose of Quintus of Smyrna's* Posthomerica

George Chapman, Ben Jonson, and John Marston's Eastward Ho! *A Retelling*

George Peele's The Arraignment of Paris: *A Retelling*

George Peele's The Battle of Alcazar: *A Retelling*

George Peele's David and Bathsheba, and the Tragedy of Absalom: *A Retelling*

George Peele's Edward I: *A Retelling*

George Peele's The Old Wives' Tale: *A Retelling*

George-a-Greene: *A Retelling*

The History of King Leir: *A Retelling*

Homer's Iliad: *A Retelling in Prose*

Homer's Odyssey: *A Retelling in Prose*

J.W. Gent.'s The Valiant Scot: *A Retelling*

Jason and the Argonauts: A Retelling in Prose of Apollonius of Rhodes' Argonautica

John Ford: Eight Plays Translated into Modern English

John Ford's The Broken Heart: *A Retelling*

John Ford's The Fancies, Chaste and Noble: *A Retelling*

John Ford's The Lady's Trial: *A Retelling*

John Ford's The Lover's Melancholy: *A Retelling*

John Ford's Love's Sacrifice: *A Retelling*

John Ford's Perkin Warbeck: *A Retelling*

John Ford's The Queen: *A Retelling*

John Ford's 'Tis Pity She's a Whore: *A Retelling*

John Lyly's Campaspe: *A Retelling*

John Lyly's Endymion, The Man in the Moon: *A Retelling*

John Lyly's Galatea: *A Retelling*

John Lyly's Love's Metamorphosis: *A Retelling*

John Lyly's Midas: *A Retelling*

John Lyly's Mother Bombie: *A Retelling*

John Lyly's Sappho and Phao: *A Retelling*

John Lyly's The Woman in the Moon: *A Retelling*

John Webster's The White Devil: *A Retelling*

King Edward III: *A Retelling*

Mankind: *A Medieval Morality Play* (A Retelling)

Margaret Cavendish's The Unnatural Tragedy: *A Retelling*

The Merry Devil of Edmonton: *A Retelling*

The Summoning of Everyman: *A Medieval Morality Play* (A Retelling)

Robert Greene's Friar Bacon and Friar Bungay: *A Retelling*

The Taming of a Shrew: *A Retelling*

Tarlton's Jests: A Retelling

Thomas Middleton's A Chaste Maid in Cheapside: *A Retelling*

Thomas Middleton's Women Beware Women: *A Retelling*

Thomas Middleton and Thomas Dekker's The Roaring Girl: *A Retelling*

Thomas Middleton and William Rowley's The Changeling: *A Retelling*

The Trojan War and Its Aftermath: Four Ancient Epic Poems

Virgil's Aeneid: *A Retelling in Prose*

William Shakespeare's 5 Late Romances: Retellings in Prose

William Shakespeare's 10 Histories: Retellings in Prose

William Shakespeare's 11 Tragedies: Retellings in Prose

William Shakespeare's 12 Comedies: Retellings in Prose

William Shakespeare's 38 Plays: Retellings in Prose

William Shakespeare's 1 Henry IV, aka Henry IV, Part 1: A Retelling in Prose

William Shakespeare's 2 Henry IV, aka Henry IV, Part 2: A Retelling in Prose

William Shakespeare's 1 Henry VI, aka Henry VI, Part 1: A Retelling in Prose

William Shakespeare's 2 Henry VI, aka Henry VI, Part 2: A Retelling in Prose

William Shakespeare's 3 Henry VI, aka Henry VI, Part 3: A Retelling in Prose

William Shakespeare's All's Well that Ends Well: A Retelling in Prose

William Shakespeare's Antony and Cleopatra: A Retelling in Prose

William Shakespeare's As You Like It: A Retelling in Prose

William Shakespeare's The Comedy of Errors: A Retelling in Prose

William Shakespeare's Coriolanus: A Retelling in Prose

William Shakespeare's Cymbeline: A Retelling in Prose

William Shakespeare's Hamlet: A Retelling in Prose

William Shakespeare's Henry V: A Retelling in Prose

William Shakespeare's Henry VIII: A Retelling in Prose

William Shakespeare's Julius Caesar: A Retelling in Prose

William Shakespeare's King John: A Retelling in Prose

William Shakespeare's King Lear: A Retelling in Prose

William Shakespeare's Love's Labor's Lost: A Retelling in Prose

William Shakespeare's Macbeth: A Retelling in Prose

William Shakespeare's Measure for Measure: A Retelling in Prose

William Shakespeare's The Merchant of Venice: A Retelling in Prose

William Shakespeare's The Merry Wives of Windsor: A Retelling in Prose

William Shakespeare's A Midsummer Night's Dream: A Retelling in Prose

William Shakespeare's Much Ado About Nothing: A Retelling in Prose

William Shakespeare's Othello: A Retelling in Prose

William Shakespeare's Pericles, Prince of Tyre: A Retelling in Prose

William Shakespeare's Richard II: A Retelling in Prose

William Shakespeare's Richard III: A Retelling in Prose

William Shakespeare's Romeo and Juliet: A Retelling in Prose

William Shakespeare's The Taming of the Shrew: A Retelling in Prose

William Shakespeare's The Tempest: A Retelling in Prose

William Shakespeare's Timon of Athens: A Retelling in Prose

William Shakespeare's Titus Andronicus: A Retelling in Prose

William Shakespeare's Troilus and Cressida: A Retelling in Prose

William Shakespeare's Twelfth Night: A Retelling in Prose

William Shakespeare's The Two Gentlemen of Verona: A Retelling in Prose

William Shakespeare's The Two Noble Kinsmen: A Retelling in Prose

William Shakespeare's The Winter's Tale: A Retelling in Prose